I0822812

Ricochet

A novel

By
J. L. Zunker

This is a work of fiction. However, the professional disciplinary proceedings described herein are based upon actual events, but all the characters and other events portrayed are either products of the author's imagination or are used fictitiously.

ISBN-13 979-8-218-26329-4

Cover design and interior formatting by Watercress Press

Printed in the United States of America by Ingram Spark and distributed by Ingram.

Published by
2Z Publishing

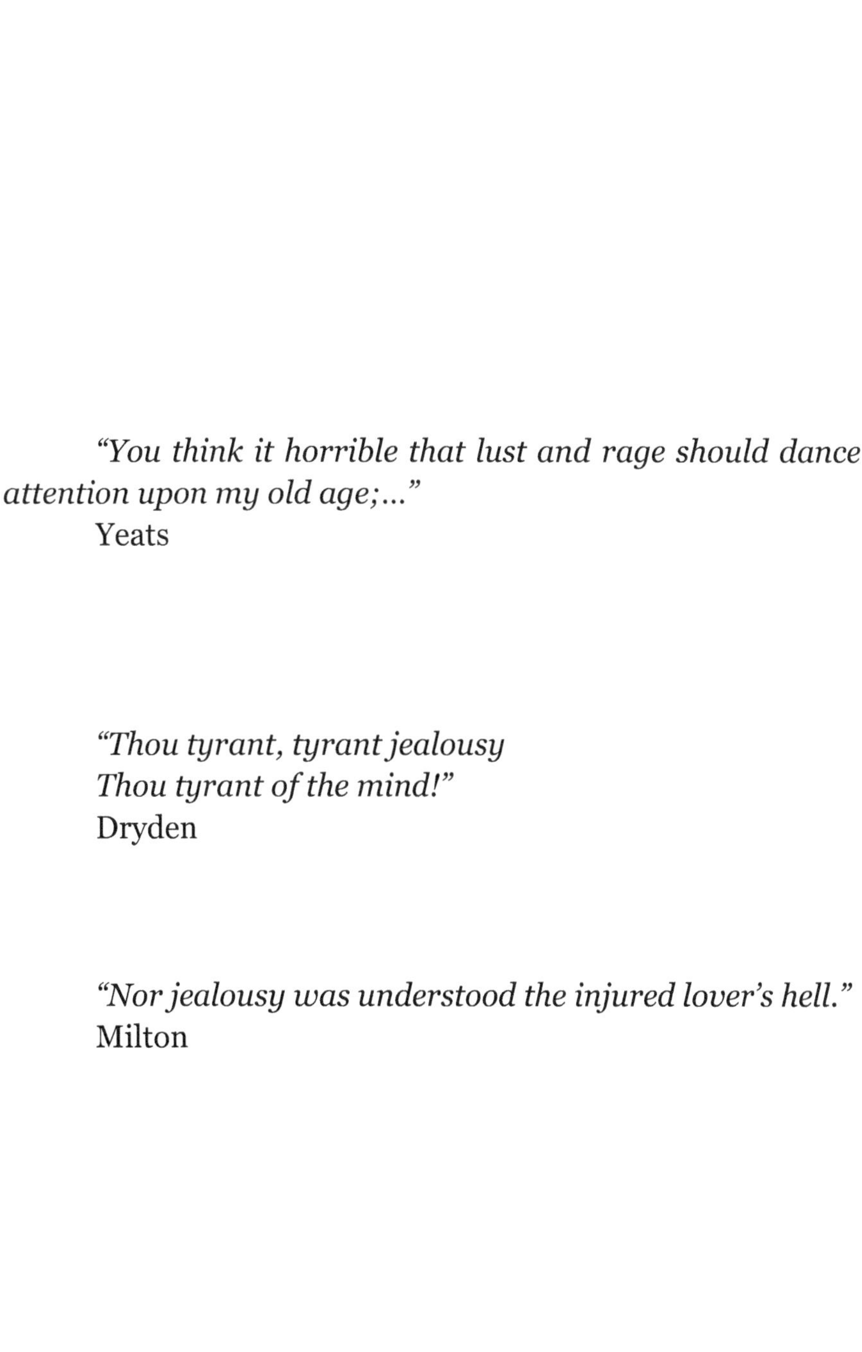

"You think it horrible that lust and rage should dance attention upon my old age;..."
Yeats

"Thou tyrant, tyrant jealousy
Thou tyrant of the mind!"
Dryden

"Nor jealousy was understood the injured lover's hell."
Milton

Dedication

For Kay, William and Pamela, my loves and bulwarks.

J. L. Zunker

Table of Contents

CAST OF MAIN CHARACTERS

Manuel Guzman - convicted murderer, temporarily confined in Bayon County jail awaiting transfer to T.D.C.
Edgar McKenzie – District Attorney of Bayon County
Tony Catalon – Sheriff of Bayon County
Mia Flores – wife of Noe Flores, mistress of McKenzie
Noe Flores – handy man, husband of Mia
El Tigre – sub-boss of South Texas for Gulf Cartel aka Emilo Zuma
Nathaniel Longfellow Keller – State Bar of Texas Prosecutor
James White – SAC FBI San Antonio Office
Thomas Hatch – FBI special agent
Jennifer Lawrence – sweetheart of Keller
Jonas Carr – State Bar Chief Disciplinary Counsel
Julia McKenzie – wife of Edgar
Jack Lewis – civil attorney for Edgar
Randy Owens – criminal defense attorney for Edgar
Joe Jackson – trial judge

Chapter 1 – The Conversation

Clump! Clump! Clump! Clump!

The sounds of the boot heels striking the concrete floor and echoing off of the low ceiling of the jailhouse corridor were clearly audible on the tape before they gradually melted away behind the steel bars that stood as mute observers. They were quickly followed by the sounds of several doors being opened and closed, more footsteps and then,

"Have a seat," said a familiar voice.

"Screw you – you son-of-a-bitch. You got a lotta nerve. You got my skinny ass sent away for twenty years and then you have that fat ass Mex drag me up here and now you want me to play palsy-walsy? We went through this the last time. Screw you."

"I thought we'd gotten through this shit last time. I understand you're pissed, but I want to help you. So, calm down. I only did what I had to do. Hell, if I'd wanted to, I could've gotten you another five or ten. The truth is you got nobody to blame but yourself. You got sloppy. It's not my fault."

"Sloppy – like shit. My lawyer was a stupid asshole and all that shit you told the jury about me poisoned their damn minds. That's why I'm here."

"Look. Believe what you want – it don't make a shit to me, but I ain't got all day to hang around here. You wanna hear what I got to offer or not?"

"I ain't heard no offer yet."

"I said I could help you. You wanna listen?"

"You know what I think? I think you're here to piss on my leg you bastard. But okay, it's hot as hell back there in that cell. It's cooler up here. Get me a Mountain Dew and I'll listen to what you got."

There was the sound of a rap on the two-way mirror in the interview room. Then, "Lonnie, can you bring us a Mountain Dew? Take this ten and keep the change." The door opens.

"You got it," said another voice as the door closes.

There was silence on the tape as the two men eyed each other and waited for the soft drink. In a few minutes there is the sound of a door opening and a voice said, "Here you go."

"Thanks Lonnie. Now if you'll give us some space, I need to talk lawyer stuff to Manuel here."

"You got it, Edgar." There was the sound of a door closing and the sound of a can being opened.

"Look, I thought you'd gotten over being pissed after our talk the other day. I came over to see if you had thought over what I'd told you, but if you're gonna keep giving me shit, I'm out of here."

The voice was distinctive and clearly recognizable by Tony Catalon the man seated at the desk and listening to the tape, as the contralto-like voice of Edgar McKenzie, the district attorney of Bayon County.

Tony Catalon, the sheriff of Bayon County made no attempt to hide the smile beginning to form on his lips. He listened to the remainder of the tape now playing out on the small cassette recorder he had been handed by Manuel Guzman.

Guzman, a freelance hit man who sometimes worked for the Gulf drug cartel, had received a twenty-year prison sentence for a homicide just six days ago. McKenzie had prosecuted the case personally. Guzman remained in the county jail awaiting transport to the Texas Department of Corrections. Two days previously he had requested an urgent meeting with the sheriff after a visit by McKenzie.

In the sheriff's office, Guzman had reported a bizarre meeting with the district attorney. In their conversation, as related by Guzman, McKenzie had promised his help in getting Guzman transported to a minimum-security prison of his choice. Furthermore, McKenzie had promised he would write to the parole board and appear on Guzman's behalf at his parole hearing. In exchange, McKenzie wanted Guzman's help in getting rid of a problem Edgar had.

Guzman told the sheriff he had asked Edgar several times to tell him about the problem and how he could help but, as Guzman stated, Edgar had turned coy and merely said for Guzman to think about his offer and what it would be worth to maybe have his time cut in half. With that, Edgar had gotten up and walked out the door.

Tony Catalon enjoyed being sheriff. In becoming sheriff, Tony had defeated McKenzie's hand-picked candidate and the two were now political enemies. More so perhaps on Tony's part than Edgar's. McKenzie, to Tony's chagrin, paid him little mind.

Still, Tony was cautious about Guzman's story. If true, he could take Edgar off the table. On the other hand, Guzman was a convicted felon who had just lost his freedom for the next twenty years, at the hands of McKenzie. It would certainly be natural for him to want revenge. Maybe all this was, was Guzman's attempt to create suspicion about some kind of possible misconduct by McKenzie.

Guzman solved Tony's dilemma by offering to wear a wire. "Wire? Hell," said the Sheriff, "We ain't got no fancy recording stuff. All I got here is this little cassette recorder."

"That'll work," said Guzman, "I'll stick it down in my boot."

The Bayon County commissioners, not being inclined to lavish county prisoners with luxuries, did not provide funds for inmate footwear. Guzman thus was able to wear his cowboy boots which indeed served as a practical hiding place for the recorder.

After inserting fresh batteries and a fresh tape into the small device, the Sheriff handed it to Guzman. "Here. Don't let anyone see it."

Guzman quickly shoved the recorder into the inside of his right boot after reassuring the Sheriff, once again, that Edgar really was up to something.

Tony now held in his hand the recording of the second meeting between Guzman and McKenzie. Tony Catalon was in his mid-fifties, of slightly more than average height. His girth; however, was outsized to his height, as were his feet, but in an opposite manner. Tony's hand-made boots, which he had a jailhouse trustee spit shine every morning, were actually made from a woman's last. His face was fleshy and his hair coal black which he combed straight back to cover his thinning scalp.

Tony Catalon had been, and still was, a wholesale beer distributor for the Valley area. His product line of Lone Star, Falstaff, Budweiser and the imported beers of Dos Equis, Carta Blanca and Tecate found a thirsty market in the area and had made Tony a fairly wealthy man. However, contrary to his expectations, his money failed to bring him the respect and prestige he craved. He had always contributed to political campaigns, usually to both sides but had never been personally involved until he filed for sheriff a year or so ago. His free beer and bar-b-que rallies won him a closely contested election over the incumbent who had been backed by McKenzie.

The race itself had been acrimonious and bruising with both sides declaring fraud. The customary post-election smiles and hand-shakes did nothing to dispel the absolute loathing each side felt toward the other.

Tony Catalon had been sheriff now for nine months and he thoroughly enjoyed every minute of it. Though he had no law enforcement experience, he regularly spoke to Rotary, Lions and women's clubs and the like, as though he were Sherlock Holmes. His crisply starched khaki uniform and the .357 mag on his hip helped sell the illusion. Tony oftentimes debated with himself whether he had gained respect or fear by his unorthodox policing. Finally, he decided that for his purposes, it made no difference, the result was the same.

Still, he envied McKenzie's public persona magnified and trumpeted by the local press. Nothing he did seemed to stack up. He gave to and sponsored local charitable events, he was an activist on law enforcement before the city council and commissioner's court, he even coached a little league football team. Nothing in the press. It really had begun to eat on him. Little did he know that McKenzie had refused to prosecute the editor of the Monitor, the local paper, when he was caught in his car on a desolate road in the company of a naked fourteen-year-old girl.

As he listened to the recording, Tony could not prevent a small smile from forming on his lips. Guzman's voice was loud and clear on the tape.

"Look. I got no reason to trust you. I ain't even sure why I'm sitting here. I don't know what your problem is and I really don't care."

"Ok, ok," said McKenzie. "I told you the other day, I appreciate where you're coming from. We've both been around the block a few times. I think we can help each other, but I ain't going no further till I think I can trust you."

"Trust me? Man, you came to me."

"Well, I got a lot more to lose than you do. But shit, ok, when I tell you I can help you, I'm not shitting. I was the governor's campaign manager down here in the Valley. I delivered the votes he needed to get elected. He owes me big time. So, hell yeah, when I say I can help you, you damn sure ought to believe it. Furthermore, if we go through with this deal, you 'll have my ass in a sling. You'll have all the leverage so I got to follow though."

"Yeah, I can see that. I guess you're right, but my butt is behind bars, how am I supposed to help?"

"Come on," said Edgar. "We both know you got friends on the outside – friends who probably owe you a favor and who aren't real skittish about how to pay it back. I know they visit you here and nobody knows what you all talk about. All I need is for you to call in a favor. That's all you gotta do."

"What kind of favor?" said the prisoner.

"Everyone in the game has guys that owe them favors. Being in the game, what do they care about what kind of favor. A favor is a favor, right?"

"You make it sound so simple. It ain't, but go ahead and lay it on me. What 'cha got?"

"Well, before this goes any further, I want you to think on this real hard cause there won't be any turning back. I gotta be sure you're locked in. I got a problem you can solve with one conversation, but I have to be sure. I'll be back in a couple of days and we'll talk some more." Said McKenzie as he moved toward the door of the small room.

"God damnit, Guzman. You got nothing." Said Catalon, as the tape played out. "You gotta get him to shit or get off the pot."

"Sheriff, I can't move him no further than he wants to go, you know that," said Guzman.

"I'm not so sure about that. I think you can push a bit," said the Sheriff. He inserted fresh batteries and a fresh tape into the recorder and handed it back to Guzman.

"Well, Sheriff, before I go putting myself out there. We need to have a talk about what's in it for me. I told you Edgar had something up his sleeve. You didn't believe me, but you heard the tape."

"Yeah, well he's up to something but no telling what yet. You get something on that tape that nails him and I promise you, we'll have a talk. So, take the recorder and get back to your cell. I gotta give a speech over at the Kiwanis."

"Lonnie, take Guzman back to his cell."

"Lonnie, where is that fat ass?"

Finally, Lonnie shuffled into the room. "Yeah, Sheriff, what's up?

"Your pension, if you don't start paying attention. Take Guzman to the back, I gotta go," said Tony, as he brushed pass Lonnie at the doorway to this office.

Chapter 2 – The Meeting

Few stars were visible. Most were obscured by smoke from the fires of Central American and Mexican farmers preparing their fields for a second planting. At ground level the smoke was not visible but it was sufficient to sting the eyes and leave the throat feeling raw. Darkness had not alleviated the heat of the day. The temperature still hovered around ninety degrees.

McKenzie's shirt stuck to his frame as he swatted mosquitos which swarmed him in legions. He leaned against the front fender of his pickup truck and could not suppress a slight shiver, even in the heat, as in the distance a forlorn train whistle competed with the serenade of the frogs in the water filled pits around the long abandoned dry hole and the mating songs of the male crickets.

McKenzie had been district attorney for sixteen years. Bayon County was his – except for that fat beer seller of a sheriff. McKenzie still couldn't figure out what happened. His people had done the usual, using names from the graveyards to vote six or seven times, using school buses to transport supporters to the polls, threatening non-supporters so they stayed away from the polls. There was no way his candidate could have lost that election. Yet, he had. Mc Kenzie didn't like what this turn of events suggested.

McKenzie himself, was in his mid-sixties, a natty dresser in his preferred dark suit and his hand-made boots. He was about six feet tall and slim with curly gray hair that he let grow long, feeling it gave him a statesman like appearance. His fair complexion was marred by childhood smallpox scars. Above his upper lip he affected a pencil thin gray mustache.

McKenzie was becoming pissed that he dare not wait in the relative comfort of his air-conditioned truck, but he knew better than to show it. The man he had been summoned to meet required a servile attitude and a non-threatening appearance. So, McKenzie waited on the almost forgotten oil field road in the middle of nowhere. He waited not without some apprehension for El Tigre, for that was who had sent the message, was as volatile as he was merciless.

After almost an hour, which seemed like days, of waiting, McKenzie heard the thump, thump of tires crossing the cattle guard and soon picked up the sound of powerful, but quiet motors. All at once he was silhouetted by the harsh beams of two vehicles traveling at high speed. One black Lincoln flashed past showering him with sand and pebbles and at about twenty yards past made a movie-like complete turn-around and came to rest with its head lights flooding him with light. Like a large black beetle, it sat there unmoving, its engine idling while the metal ticked as it cooled, and the dust quietly settled around it. There was near silence as even the insects and bull frogs rendered their obeisance. So suddenly did the rear and passenger doors open that Edgar was momentarily startled. Three heavily armed men sprang out and hastily formed a semi-circle around Edgar. Not a word was spoken.

In the meanwhile, the second car had stopped short of his pickup, its lights full upon him and its motor still purring as the dust cloud slowly subsided, two men carrying automatic weapons emerged from the left rear and passenger seat. Still there was little sound. The slamming of the car doors cut harshly through the stillness as the two armed men took up their positions.

One of the men slowly turned his body while his eyes surveyed the surrounding area. He tilted his head upwards as though sniffing the air but was instead satisfying himself there was no danger from above. Evidently, finding the situation in order, he walked to the right rear door of the second Lincoln and opened it.

A pear-shaped man of medium height with dark sunglasses covering his eyes and wearing an expensive pearl gray suit, a blindingly white shirt and a black silk tie emerged. He slowly moved toward Edgar who straightened up from his front fender and took several steps in his direction.

"Hola, mi amigo. Como esta?"

"Buenos hace tempo que no te veo."

"*Si.* But let us speak in English. My men only speak Spanish. You understand?"

"Okay," said McKenzie. "Suits me. What can I do for you?"

"I think it is more what I can do for you," said El Tigre. He continued, while making a motion to one of his men. The man went to the passenger side of the second vehicle and retrieved a cardboard box. On a nod from El Tigre, he advanced and handed it to McKenzie. "I am told you may soon have some unexpected expenses. Friends always stand by and help each other. Don't you agree?"

"Certainly, but I'm not sure what you are getting at. I've got everything under control."

"Do you? I really hope so," said the fat man. "All I'm saying is sometimes shit happens and sometimes an hombre caught up in a shitstorm forgets his friends. He panics and thinks the only way to save himself is to screw his friends. I would not like that and things I don't like usually disappear. *Comprende?"*

"*El jefe*, what's going on here? I don't know what you're talking about. There's no reason to doubt my loyalty and even less to threaten me. If I were to betray you, I would betray myself." McKenzie's voice rose to a higher octave than usual, "It ain't gonna happen."

"It is always good to be reassured. Like renewing wedding vows is it not? I have a large supply of, let's say, inventory coming in and I must be sure we understand each other. There can be no interference with this shipment. *Entiende usted?"*

With that the heavy-set man pushed up his dark glasses, which had slipped down his nose, with one hand, waved to his men with the other, whirled about and with short quick steps re-entered his automobile. Within seconds, all were gone.

Edgar was left standing as the insects and frogs resumed their serenades and the dust swirled about him. Beneath his still frozen smile, his mind was racing and he thought, *"If I ever get a chance, I'll throw that fat greaser in the pen for so long, he'll have to mail-order daylight-he's got no call to treat me this way!"*

The alliance between McKenzie and El Tigre had begun pretty much at the beginning of each of their careers. El Tigre, a former cartel assassin who had thrown in with the ultimate winner in one *of* the interminable cartel wars, had already been rewarded with South Texas while McKenzie had narrowly won his first election for district attorney. Their first meeting was sought by El Tigre and resulted in a simple, but mutually satisfactory, agreement. El Tigre would provide funds, and intimidation, where necessary, to ensure McKenzie's continuation in office. He would, from time-to-time, allow an arrest of one or more of his minions and confiscation of product. McKenzie would ensure no local law enforcement would interfere with El Tigre's operation and while he could not control the D. E. A., he would provide it with disinformation and would warn of its scheduled investigations in the local area.

Their pact had proven beneficial to both men. The defeat of McKenzie's sheriff was troubling, but not insurmountable. Catalon was not a crusader. Perhaps he couldn't be bought, but he could be out maneuvered. A change of tactics and it would be business as usual.

Getting in and starting up his truck, McKenzie crisscrossed county gravel roads on his way back to town. *What the heck set him off – what was that all about? What does he think he knows that I don't? I'd better check in with some of my boys tomorrow first thing Edgar was thinking.*

Remembering the box, he'd been handed, he pulled over to the roadside and turned on the overhead light. He used his pocketknife to cut the tape securing the box flaps. Pulling it open, he peered inside. Inside he counted fifty bundles of used ten, twenty and fifty-dollar bills. All mixed together but each bundle totaled one thousand dollars.

"Holy shit!" said McKenzie out loud. "There must really be something going on. The fat boy doesn't throw money around like this." Now Edgar really became apprehensive. There was nothing he could do until he got some intel so as he put his truck in motion, he forced himself to think of other things.

His next thoughts then were of Mia. He thought of her midnight black tresses, her ripe full breasts and her long firm legs. He felt himself begin to stir as he glanced at the dashboard clock. *Damn! It's later than I thought, he said to himself. I better not call and I'm sure as hell not crossing the river without calling her first.* Edgar had made that mistake early on in their relationship. He'd had a few drinks with a couple of the boys and was feeling horny.

Mia had stepped outside her door in response to his knock wearing only a robe with her hair all tangled. Her eyes flashed as she told him to go away and that she was not his damn property that he could just drop in on any time he needed a little sex. If he wanted to see her, he was to call first and depending on her plans, he might or might not be invited over.

Even though he was paying for her apartment and living expenses, McKenzie meekly submitted to her outburst and retreated to his truck.

Reflecting back on it now, McKenzie knew it had to be Noe. *Every time that no-good little bastard of a husband came around, who the hell knew where he went or why, Mia would welcome him back to her arms.* When Noe Flores was around, McKenzie might as well not have existed. The more he thought about it, the more his anger accelerated. His breath came in quick gasps. Pain radiated between his eyes and forehead. He nearly lost control of his truck until with a gigantic, almost physical force of will, he regained his composure.

Without consciously even going there, his thoughts turned to Julia, his wife of thirty years. She never really liked sex and for the longest time now they slept in separate rooms. He dismissed any idea of blaming her. *He was a man – an important man, he told himself. Why wasn't he entitled to happiness? No, he rapidly admitted to himself, happiness it was not.* He knew Mia did not love him. Still, he could not help himself. Obsession? Perhaps. Whatever label fit, he had to have her all to himself. To take her to bed – to lose himself in her seductive muskiness – to imagine himself even for a short while, young and strong again, was worth everything, even murder.

Chapter 3 – Bad Dreams & New Beginnings

Legs and arms thrashing, straining to breathe, nothing but red surrounding him, he was drowning in a sea of blood. Nathaniel Longfellow Keller fought himself awake amid the sweat-stained twisted sheets of his bed. Another of the now all too familiar and unwelcome dreams, not as frequent now, but still as vivid as ever. This one had been bad.

He had never shared them with anyone, somehow feeling to do so would reveal a weakness in himself. The memory presented itself as it always did.

Zero dawn . . . Sixty. Suffocating heat, endless throngs of mosquitos, the stench of the place came alive. His platoon, part of a search and destroy operation near Chu Lai, had been following a small trail in the jungle just a klick from the rice paddy where the helos had landed them when they began to receive sniper fire in their rear. As everyone dove into the underbrush, on either side of the trail, Nate suddenly fell into an unseen depression. It was at that instant that a rocket propelled grenade took off the head of his radio operator. The body remained upright as the heart pumped blood up through the mutilated torso and then it slowly folded in upon itself before collapsing onto the dirt. Verifying once again the five second life expectancy of combat radiomen in Nam. Officers and NCOs who exposed their rank fared no better.

Was it luck, providence, whatever that dictated Nate should live and the young man a few feet to his rear should die? Or, was it simply the senseless nature of war itself, Nate didn't pretend to know. He only knew, unlike a majority of combat vets, the faces of the ones he had killed did not disturb his sleep.

Only this horrific image of the untimely death of the young radio operator.

He had killed. It was not that the killing did not disturb him – it did. However, he had learned to be at peace with it. Not by trying to justify it – it was my life or his sort of thing. Rather, as shallow and simplistic as it was, Nate got by with looking at it as his job. He was trained to kill and if he was better at his job than the other guy, and he was killed, well, he just wasn't as good at his job. This was all the introspection Nate would allow himself on the subject. It was sufficient for the day – it allowed him to maintain his outward veneer of stoicism.

Nate was shaken to his core after the death of his parents, just before his college graduation. Not only was he now totally alone but without funds or prospects. The forced sale of the heavily mortgaged family farm netted him barely enough to pay off his college debts. Under the circumstances, the Army seemed to offer a return of order and stability into his life. Besides he probably was going to be drafted anyway. Might as well get on with it.

After basic training, his application for OCS was eagerly accepted by the army which was losing junior officers almost faster than it could produce them. So off to Fort Benning and officer candidate and basic officer leader courses. He was then deemed to be not only an officer candidate and a gentleman but a leader of men. He was not yet twenty-three and the next stop on his young life's journey was the Republic of South Vietnam.

There he found, as he had expected, the ugly cacophony of war, but unexpectedly giant scorpions, cobras, vipers, fifteen hundred species of plants, many of them decidedly unpleasant, oppressive heat, life sucking diseases and for a large part, an unfriendly populace.

He was assigned a platoon in company A, 2nd Battalion, 11th Infantry Brigade, 23rd (Americal) Division. The 11th had less than a glorious reputation. In fact, it was known as the "butcher brigade". Years before Nate's posting, a certain Lt. Calley had directed one of its platoons in the massacre of three to four hundred Vietnamese civilians in the small village of My Lai.

Later, its commander, a brigadier general, was charged with, but acquitted of murder for shooting civilians from his helicopter. Nate had no illusions about war. He had read somewhere that in the 3400 years of recorded history humans had been at peace for only 268 of them. He recalled thinking to himself, while he had accepted war in general and Nam, in particular, as being abhorrent, his assignment to this unit made his situation even worse.

With a head dulled and aching now due to his aborted slumber, and a body rebelling against his commands, Nate forced himself from the bed. He crept to the nearby chair to retrieve his draped jeans. Ever so slowly he stood on one leg and then the other as he pulled up his trousers. Barefoot he made it to the bathroom, relieved himself, swallowed half a hand full of aspirin and headed for the kitchen in the small house he rented in East Austin.

As he approached his coffee maker on the counter in front of him, he had to skip aside to avoid stepping on a dead lizard. *Cat's rent payment*, he thought as he dumped the small still carcass into the garbage.

Cat was an orange and white male cat of indeterminable breed that had entered his life a short while ago. Nate had discovered Cat's almost lifeless body, bloody with a torn and ragged ear, lying huddled in front of his garage door one night as he returned from work.

Nate, which was the name he answered to, was not a cat man. Point of fact, he was not a pet man. However, he could not just leave the cat to its fate. So, he drove it to the nearest veterinary clinic. After entrusting the cat to the receptionist Nate took a seat in the waiting room. After about thirty or forty minutes he heard his name being called. He looked toward the sound and saw a blonde tech in green scrubs with a clip board. As she approached, his initial appraisal was reinforced. Five foot three or four, about one ten or one fifteen pounds, open face, sun burnished skin, the baggy scrubs obscured her figure, but he figured it had to be as good as the parts of her he could see. She smiled a dazzling smile, that almost sent Nate to his knees, and held out her small hand. Nate took it almost reverently. He forgot to let it go as he made contact with her dark green eyes.

He was embarrassed and flustered as she had to pointedly withdraw her hand. She seemed to take no notice as she explained that the vet had mended the cat's ear and cleaned it up. It would be fine and he would be able to take it home in ten or fifteen minutes.

Over the clinic's FM radio, Jerry Jeff Walker was singing... "*Home to the Armadillo... the friendliest people and the prettiest women you've ever seen...*" *Isn't it so*, thought Nate.

"I'd like to have the name of your cat for our records," she said. Abruptly brought back to his senses, Nate stammered that it wasn't his cat and explained how he came to bring it to the clinic.

"That's really kind of you," she said. "But what are you going to do with it now, are you going to keep it? The reason I ask is because he is going to need some care for a while or are you going to take him to the animal shelter? We really don't do that so it would be up to you. The shelter is usually pretty crowded so I don't know if they'll have room. The thing is, if they are too crowded, they'll just put the cat to sleep."

Nate instantly knew he could not chance that, so against his better judgment he decided then and there to take the cat home with him. This process also aided in his desire to prolong the conversation. So, Nate said, "No, that's okay, I'll take him with me."

"That's nice of you, but you don't strike me as a cat person. Are you sure? Well, maybe your wife is a cat person."

"I'm not married. I grew up on a farm so I think I can handle it. By the way, my name is Nate."

"I'm Jennifer, Jennifer Lawrence," she said smiling, "everyone calls me Jen. If you've never played nurse maid to a cat before I have to warn you, it takes a lot of patience." Nate explained that his mother had a cat on the farm when he was growing up so that should help him handle things.

Jen didn't seem convinced but as it was his choice, she simply smiled showing a lot of white teeth. Then she asked if he knew whether or not the cat had its shots. Nate told her he didn't think so since it was a stray but to go ahead and give it whatever it needed. He demurred when Jen asked if he wanted the cat "fixed". Nate was very clear that this cat deserved to remain as it was.

Jen, much to Nate's wishes, did not seem in a rush to go into the back. She said, "so you grew up on a farm. Wide open spaces. That must have been wonderful. I grew up in Dallas. I'm afraid I'm a city girl."

Nate had already noticed she had no rings on her fingers. So, he said, "Dallas, eh. What brings you to Austin?"

"Well, I'm in veterinary school at A&M and I've taken an internship here in order to make some money to finish out school and to get some hands-on work experience. After I got my undergraduate degree in education, I decided I didn't want to be a teacher so I kind of started over. My parents weren't too happy about it so I'm sort of doing it on my own. How about you?"

"Well, long story short, I'm a lawyer working for the State Bar of Texas. I prosecute lawyers for professional misconduct," said Nate.

"Really? That sounds interesting. I truly would like to hear more, but I've got to get back to my job. Would you let me take a rain check on that?" she said with a lovely sincere smile. She reached out and touched his arm and she was gone.

Nate found himself with a smile on his face, but also a strange aching in his gut. Before he could decode it all, his name was called by the receptionist. He was handed a cardboard box with the cat apparently sleeping inside and a statement for services, a sheet of instructions and a bottle of antibiotics. No one told him how he was going to get the cat to swallow the pills.

Standing there at the desk, Nate admitted to himself that he had inadvertently set in motion one and maybe two relationships. He was, as yet, weighing each but knew in his heart the "yeas" would probably prevail if it came to a vote.

He then and there decided to definitely keep the tom cat. Maybe the cat had already decided to move in with him. No matter, here he was. Now he needed a name. Not having any experience in cat naming Nate decided to just call him "Cat." Nate realized this showed a lack of imagination but, upon a brief reflection realized that one, the animal wouldn't care, and two, probably wouldn't response no matter what he was called.

Over the next several weeks he and Cat established boundaries. Cat was the master and Nate his servant. As Cat regained his health his demands to be let outside the house and to be re-admitted at odd hours became a problem. So, Nate with the agreement of this landlord, removed the hollow core back door and replaced it with a solid wooden door. In addition to the door, he purchased at a nearby Home Depot a saw, some hinges and screws. Though he was not a craftsman by any means, but being a farm boy, Nate had enough skills to install a cat door for Cat. The landlord supplied the paint. So, then Cat could come and go as he pleased. Cat had a territory to patrol, and he took his job seriously and, if on his rounds he happened upon a willing female, well, wasn't that a warrior's due? He healed and grew swiftly, and he eagerly took on any male cat that had the temerity to encroach upon his ground. Few tried again. Cat, it appeared, was utterly without fear and earned Nate's parent-like pride.

Cat would take on anything. He took his lumps but remained unchanging in his self-appointed duty. Even so far as taking on a Labrador that its owner had unleashed which wandered on to Nate's small front yard. The lab, though admittedly not full grown, still outweighed the cat by twenty pounds or more. No matter, it simply had no clue as to how to deal with ten or eleven pounds of orange and white hissing and clawing fury.

Nate was taken aback when the dog's owner pounded on his door. The open door revealed a rather overweight female, red-faced, breathing heavily with a rather large dog in her arms. She was wearing a red blouse and a pair of blue shorts with large white polka dots. The shorts were stretched about to their limits and looked as though they may have belonged to her younger, smaller sister, three or four years ago.

"Yes," asked Nate.

"Does that awful orange cat belong to you?" she asked. Nate told her he disagreed with the "awful" part but in so far as the cat belonged to anyone, he supposed it belonged to him.

"Well," said the woman, still breathing heavily, "Your cat attacked my dog! What are you going to do about it?"

"Let's see," Nate replied, "Your dog was on my lawn, he was not on a leash in violation of the city ordinance, he outweighed the cat by twenty or more pounds, and you want to complain? I tell you what I think, I'll give Cat a treat tonight."

"Well, I never! Screw you, you asshole," the corpulent woman managed in an indigent squeal. This while she was saluting Nate with the middle finger of her right hand.

"Thanks for your kind thought. Have a nice day," Nate said while closing his door. As he moved further into the hallway, he spotted Cat entering through the back cat door. He was strutting around and appeared to be rather pleased with himself. Cat paused, then quickly presented Nate with a rather smug look before trotting off to the bedroom where he jumped upon the edge of the bed and promptly fell asleep. Totally indifferent to the ruckus he had caused.

Nate finished his coffee, dressed and, after replenishing Cat's water and food dishes went out his front door, locked it behind him, got into his gently used BMW, the only thing he had salvaged from his divorce, and drove north on the IH35 frontage road to work.

Chapter 4 – Pleasant Complications

As to Jen, an unexpected, but more welcome relationship had sprung up. It began the evening after the trip to the vet. Nate had just gotten home from work and was crushing an antibiotic to place in the cat's food when there was a knock on his door. He opened the door to find Jen standing there holding a cat litter box, bag of cat litter and a bag of cat food. Nate swiftly changed his expression from surprise to welcome.

Jen's color was heightened by her blush as she timidly uttered, "Oh I – oh, I thought I should check on the patient." Nate quickly took her packages and wondered if he had ever seen anyone so lovely and so disarmingly innocent at the same time. She still had her scrubs on, her hair pulled up and no makeup. Nate could not help himself, he simply stared. She began to move back from the door, obviously uncomfortable under his gaze. She began to apologize saying, "I didn't mean to barge in on you. I'll just leave these things I thought you would need for the cat. I'll just go now." Her face had turned a darker hue of pink.

Nate, he thought to himself, *You fool, you can't let this one get away.* "No, no," he said, "please come in. It's just that I don't get many visitors. Please forgive me. Sometimes it takes a while for my brain to engage. The cat's right over there. Thanks for the food and stuff."

"You're welcome," she said. "You sure I'm not intruding?"

"Cross my heart."

Jen meanwhile had moved over and knelt by the cat which was lying on a bath towel in the kitchen. She softly stroked his head and was rewarded by a weak wag of his tail and a lick of her hand.

"Look at that guy, hitting on you," said Nate. "When I went to pet him, he bared his teeth."

"Well, he probably wasn't feeling too great. Also, sometimes petting can be painful to cats. Each sort of has its own place to be petted so you first have to be patient and feel it out. He's looking a lot better. Did you have any trouble getting him to take his medicine?"

"No, I just crushed them up and put them in his food. I guess he was hungry, he just gobbled it all up."

"Look, I know my gawking made you uncomfortable. I am so sorry – it's just... won't you sit down; can I get you something to drink? I really would feel like an idiot if my rudeness ran you off, please stay awhile."

Jen looked around. There were a couple of stools at the kitchen divider, a worn steno chair at a rather battered oak desk in the living room, along with a recliner and a small television on a metal cart. At the wall nearest the recliner was Nate's record player and record collection in a cabinet.

Nate, now even more embarrassed, said, "I have to apologize for the lack of seats, but truth is, I don't have any visitors, so it hasn't been a problem. But here, try this stool, I don't think it's too uncomfortable." *I need to get some furniture*, he thought to himself.

"Well," said Jen as she smiled, "I wouldn't want to make you feel like an idiot. I guess I can stay a few minutes. It would not be kind of me if I made you feel bad. Besides, I do have that rain check to collect on. You were going to tell me about your job. It sounded interesting."

Nate didn't much want to talk about himself, but he had made up his mind when he saw her at his door that he would do whatever it took to keep Jen in his presence as long as he could.

So, Nate began, "As I told you I work for the State Bar of Texas. It's a state agency of the judicial branch of the state government, even though it receives no state funds – it's supported largely by the dues of the lawyers licensed in Texas. In order to practice law in Texas a lawyer has to be a member of the State Bar. The bar has adopted rules, approved by the state supreme court, that lawyers have to comply with. When a lawyer in Texas is accused of violating those rules, the bar's office of disciplinary counsel, where I work, is required to prosecute that attorney. Under Texas rules an accused attorney, unlike in the other forty-nine states, can request a jury trial. That's where I come in. I try jury trials all over the state."

"I had no idea. I never knew that," she said.

"Well," said Nate, "That's my teachable moment and now I want to hear about you."

"Oh, no you don't," she said, "I've still got some of that rain check to cash in. Tell me about yourself."

"You know," Nate said, "that may be the scariest phrase in the English language, at least to me. There's not much to tell and I think what there is to tell is boring."

"No sir, you owe me," said Jen.

"Well," Nate began reluctantly, "I've already told you I grew up on a black land farm in Central Texas."

"Wait, wait, I don't even know your full name, start with that," said Jen.

"It's Nathaniel Longfellow Keller, so now you know why I go by Nate."

"I like that. Impressive. How did you come by that?"

"My father farmed, and my mother taught high school literature. I guess she admired Henry Wadsworth Longfellow and Nathaniel Hawthorne. I'm just thankful she didn't name me 'Hiawatha'," said Nate with a smile.

"I still like it, now go on."

"So, I went to a small teacher's college just down the road. Just weeks before graduation, my parents were killed in a one car accident near Beaumont. They were on their way to visit one of my mom's cousins that was seriously ill. The DPS report said there was a terrific wind and rainstorm and fog, and the supposition was the car left the pavement and ended upside down in a deep ditch."

"Oh Nate, I'm so sorry."

"It's been a long time ago now, but at the time, as a twenty-one-year-old, and the only child, with no close relatives, I admit, I was hit pretty hard. Anyway, I graduated and with the help of the bank, it held the mortgage, I sold the farm and was able to pay off my student loans. That was about as far as the money went. So, there I was with a BA in government, no proper employment with that degree, no funds and, as they say, my future wasn't looking too bright. I decided then to do what a lot of desperate guys my age were doing, I joined the Army. I was going to be drafted anyway so all I really did was to cut out the waiting time."

"Anyway, I was sent off to Vietnam. I survived without a scratch, more or less, came back to Texas, entered UT law school, got married, got divorced, lost my job with her daddy's law firm in Houston, returned to Austin, and so here I am."

"Any children?"

"No, neither of us wanted any at that time."

"You've had a full life already compared to me. You seem to be happy now and I'm glad for you. But I think I've used up my rain check and besides I've got an early shift tomorrow, so I need to get back to my place," Jen said.

"Well look, I'm happy you came by and I thank you for the cat stuff. Can I see you again?"

"I hope so," she said opening the door. "You know where I work."

After she left, Nate pondered. *A cat and maybe a girlfriend, my life is getting crowded. Isn't that nice!* He went to his kitchen, threw a couple of ice cubes in a glass and poured himself a good-sized drink of Boodles. He went to his record player, searched through his records, settled on one and placed it on the turntable. He sat down in his recliner, took a swallow of gin, leaned back with satisfaction as he was surrounded by Bunny Berigan's 'I Can't Get Started'. Nate could never choose his favorite horn player. Bix Beiderbecke, though he played coronet, had an innovative driving style, or Berigan's superb, round tone on the trumpet. Why choose? Nate was an aficionado of both along with others like Louis Armstrong, Ray Eldridge and King Oliver.

As he settled in, Nate had to wonder at the phoenix-like manner in which his life had suddenly been resurrected. He was slightly troubled by his response to Jen's query. He hadn't been dishonest with her. What he told her was the truth about his life. He just hadn't supplied some of the details. He was not much given to introspection but the prospect of entering into a new and perhaps intimate relationship seemed to open the floodgates of his memory.

He had met Leslie in UT Law School where he had enrolled, pursuant to the GI Bill, after his release from the Army and his return to Texas. Leslie was a stunner – no one could deny that. She was the queen of the law school – smart as she was pretty. He was certainly aware of her in his first-year law class. The student body and classes were small compared to the undergraduate school, so it was not unusual that by the middle of the first-year everyone knew everyone else. It was in the second year when they were in law review together and worked on several research projects that the two of them gravitated into becoming a couple.

Nate was flattered by her attention, by her long blonde hair, her striking features and her sensuous body, to say nothing of her mind, which he knew was at least the equal, if not superior, to his own. He did wonder sometimes what she saw in him, but he quickly dismissed the thought. Why look a gift horse in the mouth?

He asked her to marry him. Looking back, he wasn't sure if he loved her or whether he was simply dazzled by the sheer wonder of it all. They were both honor students. They married after graduation and passage of the bar exam. They then went to work in her father's silk-stocking law firm in Houston; he in the litigation section and she in estate planning and probate.

Nate could hardly believe his good fortune. He worked tirelessly and was rewarded by raises and more complex litigation files. Not exactly rags to riches but to a farm boy, the substantial salary, big new house, foreign cars, entrance to exclusive clubs, all were beyond his modest dreams of just being an attorney to help people.

His work ethic enabled him to generally bill seventy or so hours a week. However, he soon began to clash with the managing partner who kept pushing him to increase his billing. Unspoken, but clearly implied, was the notion that it did not matter whether he actually worked all the hours he was expected to charge out. Nate was repelled by the practice.

A sad joke was floating around the firm. A young lawyer is admiring a new Ferrari being shown him by a senior partner. The young man gushing over it and the partner tells him all he has to do is work hard and turn in his billable hours. "Gosh," says the young lawyer, "if I do that, you mean one day I can buy a car like that?" "No," says the partner, "Then I can buy the newest model."

The dispute over billing chafed Nate but, as he came to realize, the main source of his disillusionment was the firm's clients and their officers. These were self-satisfied men who drew millions in salary and millions more in annual bonuses who never flinched at the harm their corporate products caused. Whether it was polluting the streams with their factory run – off, dirtying the air with the smoke from their fossil fueled factories or causing children to choke on their defective toys, they were all the same. They turned to Nate to defend them. When he won, as he usually did, they did not acknowledge his advocatory skills for the result. Rather, they treated the verdict as proof that they were in the right all along. After all, didn't the first Roosevelt say that the business of America was business?

Nate had never been much of a drinker. When he did drink it was usually a beer. Now though, he found himself stopping at a bar on the way home to have a drink. At first, he told himself it was just to let the traffic clear out. But then one drink led to two and then to more and Nate found himself driving home in a haze, missing dinner, forgetting invitations to join friends – his relationship with Leslie was starting to unravel. He tried to explain to her about the pressure he felt about the billing, clients' lack of appreciation, the unspoken but still present burden of measuring up as the son-in-law of the firm founder. He tried numerous times to explain all of this to Leslie. The breach between them grew wider when she defended the firm, its policies and its clients and was dismissive of his insecurity about her father's expectations.

Nate loathed himself for the weakness his resort to alcohol had exposed. But the more he despised the habit the more he drank. He knew he was headed for self-destruction – not that he wanted to go there – but his foot was already heavy on the pedal, like it or not, and he was headed full speed in that direction.

That Christmas, they were at the home of Leslie's father and all the firm's partners, associates, staff and their spouses or dates were present for the party. After several hours or so into the party and after Nate had on several occasions visited the open bar and during one of the inevitable lulls, that seem to occur at precisely the wrong time in most gatherings, Nate barked out, "Stop feeling me up, get your hands off me, you old bitch." This was directed at a most senior partner's prune-faced wife who had a well-earned reputation as a cougar.

The husband, florid of face and more than a little under the influence himself, staggered slightly as he pushed his way through the crowd to place himself in front of Nate. In a slightly slurred voice, he demanded, "Who are you calling a bitch?"

"You heard me," countered Nate, also in a somewhat slurred voice.

"I demand an apology."

"You're not getting one."

With that the partner made a wild swing at Nate who easily avoided it and responded with a quick jab to his opponent's chin. The man dropped to the floor like a rock dropped down a well. Whereupon Nate was pushed and grabbed at by several bystanders. Just as the scene was about to ascend into a brawl, Leslie's father, in an authoritative voice, shouted, "Stop it! Break it up!" The partygoers responded. They backed away from Nate as others helped the downed partner to his feet and supported him as he made his way to the bar.

The room went totally silent, and the party ended for Nate rather abruptly after that. Leslie and her father half pushed, half carried him out the door and into his car.

As Leslie drove off, Nate tried to explain. "I told that woman at least three times I wasn't interested and to get her hands off me. It wasn't my fault that the room went quiet just as I told her again. I mean what would you have done if her husband had been rubbing your ass?"

"Well, he wasn't, was he?" said Leslie. "And if he was, I would not have made an awful scene, I would have moved away from him and avoided it. He was as drunk as you. Do you understand who he is? He's my supervising attorney. Do you think he is not going to retaliate against me? You've ruined my career."

"Come on, Les, that's nonsense, you're overreacting. It's your daddy's firm, nothing is going to happen to your career. Look, I'll apologize tomorrow and blame it on too much to drink and the whole thing will blow over."

"Is that what you think? If so, you have no idea what you've done. I can't help you."

"Can't or won't?"

There was no response. Leslie drove in silence the rest of the way to their home. At home Leslie announced that he would not be sleeping in her bed. The next morning, Nate awoke at mid-morning in the guest room with the mother of all headaches. He was alone. Leslie had gone to work. Finally, close to noon, Nate had gathered himself together somewhat and made his way to the office. No one spoke to him and they uniformly avoided any eye contact. In his office he discovered his personal possessions tossed into a banker's box. A letter on firm stationary signed by the managing partner informed him his services were no longer required, enclosed was a check for his monthly salary plus two weeks for severance pay. A security guard had been summoned by someone and he was escorted to the door after giving up his keys.

Whatever fog remained in Nate's mind evaporated quickly and a shudder went through his body. Man, he thought, I've really screwed up this time. He didn't know how badly.

As he parked his car and walked to his front door, he was met by an attorney he knew only slightly who specialized in family law. Rick, that was his name, Nate couldn't remember his last name and greeted him rather sheepishly.

"Nate, I'm sorry about this, it's nothing personal but Leslie has filed for divorce. Rather than have you served, I asked her if I could talk to you first. Leslie is sure about this. Maybe her old man is pushing her, I don't know, but she appears adamant to me. You are free to take your clothes and anything else you care to but after that I have a temporary restraining order."

Nate stared numbly ahead as though Rick's words were directed to someone else. He stood mute for long minutes before appearing to gather himself. He asked, "Leslie doesn't even want to talk to me – give me a chance to explain?"

"Afraid not. Maybe we should go inside and sit down."

Nate allowed himself to be led into his own house. In the living room he was introduced to a young lady, who Rick explained was a member of his staff and a notary public. Nate didn't catch her name.

"Nate," said Rick as they seated themselves in facing armchairs in the living room. "I know you understand how this works, we've filed as a 'no fault'. The two of you have almost no equity in your home, you can keep your car, you all have separate bank accounts, you can keep yours, so unless you want to fight over the furniture, there's really nothing else. Neither of you have retirement accounts yet. I've got a copy of the divorce petition and a waiver for you to sign. If you'll let me know your new address, I'll mail you a copy of the decree."

Another long pause, neither of them saying anything, until Nate brought his head up and nodded. Rick handed him the waiver and a fountain pen. Nate signed. The young lady signed and placed her seal on it, and it was done. Nate packed his clothes, a few personal items, books, records, etc., got into his car and drove off. He did not look back.

He had no destination. He simply stopped at the first motel on South Main that had a bar. He spent the next several weeks drinking and angry. Then he began feeling sorry for himself, wrapped tightly in self-pity until one day, there was nothing he could recall afterwards that ignited it, he just decided to stop. He quit drinking, began eating, and after a while he began to feel like his old self. Having time on his hands, he was looking through a month-old Texas Bar Journal he had found in his briefcase, and he noticed an ad for a trial attorney in the office of the Chief Disciplinary Counsel. The application period did not close for several days. He decided to go to Austin and check it out.

Chapter 5 – The Plot

A few days after his last conversation with McKenzie, Guzman's brooding boredom was interrupted by Lonnie banging on the door of his cell. "Get your lazy butt over here. Edgar wants to talk to you."

Guzman swung his legs off his bunk and managed to shift the recorder around in his boot so he could get his foot in without Lonnie seeing. Guzman, escorted by Lonnie, entered into the interview room where Edgar was waiting. Lonnie held out his palm which Edgar filled with a twenty-dollar bill, "Let me know when you all are finished," said Lonnie as he retreated down the hallway.

"Have you thought about our talk?" asked Edgar.

"Yeah, so long as all I gotta do is talk to somebody, I'm in. So, let's get on with it."

"Well, here's the thing. There's a little shit-ass Mexican by the name of Noe something or the other that keeps going across the river and messing with my stuff."

"How's he messing with your stuff?"

"Don't make no difference to you. I want him put down. Can you arrange that?"

"Man, that's some serious shit."

"Well can you, or can't you?"

"I wanna be sure we understand each other. You want this guy dead?"

"Yeah, I want his ass terminated – Is that going to be a problem? You people kill each other all the time. Every few days or so a body washes up on the riverbank. It's not like you have to dirty your hands. All you gotta do is call in a favor."

"Man, that's some favor. But, yeah, I can check with a couple guys. I'll need some time though."

"It don't have to be tomorrow, but I don't want it weeks or months either. Here's a mug shot of the guy from when he was arrested for drunk. I've written his addresses on the bottom. I can see your cell window from my office. When it's done, hang a pair of jeans in your window and I'll come over as soon as I can. Get some identification off the guy to prove it's done, OK?"

"Shouldn't be a problem."

"See you then," said McKenzie as he got up and moved through the door.

Shortly after McKenzie left, Guzman insisted to Lonnie that he had to see the Sheriff. Lonnie, being Lonnie, left Guzman alone in the interrogation room as he slow walked, his top speed, up to the sheriff's office. Upon receiving instructions to do so, Lonnie sauntered to the small room and retrieved Guzman. The two of them then slow walked to the sheriff's office, taking time out for a stop by the alcove containing the vending machines. Lonnie selected a Baby Ruth candy bar for himself and turned to Guzman who shook his head. They resumed their turtle-like pace to the sheriff's door. Upon knocking and receiving permission to enter, the two of them stood on frayed carpet before the sheriff's desk.

"God damn it, Lonnie. How can it take you twenty, God damn, minutes to walk a few feet and back? And take that God damn candy bar out of your face when I'm talking to you! You got a prisoner there, act like a God damned law officer!"

"Yes, sir. Sorry Sheriff," muttered Lonnie, pulling the remainder of the candy bar from his mouth while turning away to hide the stream of chocolate that dripped from his mouth onto the front of his uniform shirt.

Catalon rose from his chair, his face turning beet red, he struggled to shout to Lonnie to get his fat ass out of his office before collapsing back into his chair.

Guzman waited while Catalon finally composed himself. He placed the recorder on Tony's desk, saying, "I think this is what you were waiting for."

Guzman and Catalon listened to the recorder. Each aware of its implications.

"Sheriff, I ain't gonna go through with this," said Guzman.

"Oh yes you will, but we'll fake it, you'll see. Now I got things to do. You find Lonnie and get back to your cell."

Catalon sat at his desk mulling over his options. Finally, he shouted to his secretary and told her to call the FBI in San Antonio and make an appointment with the agent in charge.

The Next Afternoon

Catalon presented himself at the front desk of the San Antonio FBI office and was shortly greeted by James White, the SAC. After swapping greetings and some more or less desultory twaddle, White asked Catalon what was on his mind. Like a magician pulling a rabbit from a hat, Catalon pulled the recorder and two cassettes from his inside coat pocket. With a flourish he laid them on White's desk and leaned back in his chair with a contented smile.

"What the hell is that?" demanded White.

"That, Mr. FBI man, is your ticket to a promotion. I know how much you feds like taking down state officials. Well, I'm handing you the district attorney down in my county all tied up with a red ribbon."

White rolled his eyes as if to say, Lord, save me from these local yokels. Nevertheless, with Catalon's assurance that these tapes showed some serious crimes, White listened to both tapes. As he listened, his initial skepticism was replaced by the realization that perhaps this sheriff from South Texas wasn't wasting his time. As the last tape played out, White leaned over and pushed the intercom button. "Tom, can you come to my office?"

Directly came the reply. "Sure, boss be right there."

In a few minutes in walked a fit young man in his early thirties, of slightly above average height with a ruddy complexion and blond hair.

"Tom, this is sheriff Tony Catalon of Bayon County. He's brought us an interesting tape on the local district attorney. Sheriff Catalon, this is special agent Thomas Hatch. I'm going to assign him to this case, and I wanted the two of you to meet. Ok, thanks Tom. I'll be briefing you later." Tom left the office, his expression impassive and White continued, as the door closed behind him. "Tom's a specialist in surveillance and recording. I'll have him report to you tomorrow morning. Now, I know he looks young but he's a Marine with combat experience in Viet Nam. He may be quiet-voiced and he doesn't curse but believe me, he is totally reliable and tough. I guess I should add that he's a Morman. But, he likes his beer so the two of you should get along just fine. And, before you ask, he only has one wife."

"Well," said Catalon, "I guess a man only needs one wife and one girl friend," and he laughed out loud.

Ignoring Catalon's attempt at humor, White continued, "What we'll do is wire up the jailbird and we'll get ahold of this Noe kid and get some ID off him. Then we'll feed it to your D.A. on the wire. My guess is he'll go for the sting and say some things when he thinks this Noe is dead that will be a confession or as close to one as we'll need. Then we'll have him," said White while slapping Tony on the back and showing him to the door. "Sheriff, its good cops like you that help us do our job."

Catalon's chest swelled with pride, apparently never realizing how unceremoniously he had been shown to the door.

Next Day at the Sheriff's Office in Eisenberg

As promised, Hatch appeared the next day. He had Guzman brought up and he went through the process of installing and explaining the workings of the transmitting equipment. All Guzman had to do was press a place on his chest for it to begin. Hatch removed the equipment and Guzman was escorted back to his cell.

"The FBI has issued an APB for Noe," said Hatch. "So, The FBI, the Border Patrol, federal marshals, the local police and your deputies are all on the lookout for Noe. We're keeping it just with law enforcement, no media. We don't want McKenzie alerted."

"Well," said Catalon, "my office has received a tip that he's expected to do yardwork out close to Edgar's house. I've had deputies staked out in the neighborhood waiting to see if he shows."

"Sounds good," said Hatch. "I'll hang around until the sting is over. I've left my motel number with your dispatcher."

Finally, almost, a week later Catalon called Hatch. “Agent Hatch this is Sheriff Catalon, my boys just grabbed Noe, they’re bringing him to the station as we speak.”

“Great, I’m on my way.”

As Hatch arrived at the sheriff's headquarters, he was motioned to the sheriff's private office. There he found Catalon saying to Noe. “I know you can’t quite get your head around it yet, but it's true. McKenzie is trying to arrange a hit on you. We need you to trap him.”

“I ain’t done nothin to Edgar, why would he want to kill me? I can’t stop the slimy bastard from messing with my Mia. He pays me no mind. He don’t need to kill me.”

Hatch interjected, saying, “I’m special agent Tom Hatch. May I call you Noe?”

Noe noded.

“We will keep you safe, just trust us. If you’ll loan us your driver’s license, we’ll do all the rest and if you agree, the U.S. government will put you up in a hotel in San Antonio until all this is over. *Comprende?”*

“Yeah, I guess so, here’s my Texas and Mexican drivers' licenses. What about my lawnmower?”

Catalon interrupted, “Don’t worry about tha*t,* we’ll get it, and we'll keep it for you. Okay? Thank you, Noe. The deputy over there will drive you to San Antonio,” said the Sheriff.

A pair of blue jeans were stuck in Guzman’s cell window, and everyone sat down to wait. Several hours later, Edgar appeared and met Guzman in the interrogation room. The recording of their conversation was crystal clear.

“I got your signal and came as soon as I could. Is it over?”

“Yeah, it’s done. My boys told me the little bastard squealed like a pig at the end. Begging for his life.”

"I don't really want to hear all that. Is he gonna be found?"

"Nah, the guys took him way out in the desert and buried him. The coyotes ain't even gonna find him. Here, this is his ID you wanted," said Guzman.

McKenzie's face blanched as he fingered the documents. After a while, he said in a hoarse low voice, "You know it's too bad, but what the hell, he was a no-good little sum bitch anyway." With that he let himself out of the room, turning to say, "Hang tight, I'll get back to you."

The wire recordings and the documents were hand carried by Hatch back to San Antonio where the recordings were transcribed. Everything was marked and placed in the safe by Hatch. The next day, Hatch drove them to the U.S. Attorney in Brownsville.

Chapter 6 – The Assignment

Months later, as Nate entered the State Bar Office, the pleasant lady guarding the tomb told him the boss wanted to see him.

The boss was Jonas Carr, the Chief Disciplinary Counsel. Jonas was only months away from retirement and office scuttlebutt had it that Nate was his designated successor. Nate had heard the rumors and did what he could to squelch them. He was conflicted, he wasn't sure he was ready to swap the courtroom for a largely administrative position. Then, on the other hand, Jonas had pretty much given him a free hand. There was no way to know how Nate might fare with a successor. One thing for sure, he couldn't stand to be micro-managed, and he did not tolerate fools or their rules.

Carr's office door was open, and Nate entered saying, "Morning Jonas, Nickey said you wanted to see me."

Morning, Nate! Yes, I've got something for you. Have a seat. Coffee?"

Carr was of medium height, florid of face, bald except for gray hair around his ears and the back of his head which he kept closely trimmed. Cooking was his hobby and one look at him was enough to know he enjoyed his culinary creations. Jonas was soft spoken but anyone who underestimated his backbone soon learned never to do so again. He was possessed of a good legal mind and an intuitive skill that allowed him to navigate the political waters with the Supreme Court, the State Bar Board of directors, the media, and the Bar's membership, all without sullying his integrity. His relationship with Nate verged on parental.

"Watch the game Saturday?" Carr asked as he turned to his coffee maker behind his desk. Carr was so particular about his coffee he had his own machine.

"Watched it on TV," said Nate. "Looks like Ackers has the makings of a pretty good team this year."

"Looks like it; just wish he had a little more offense. Those 3-0 and 6-0 games are hard on my nerves. Here's your coffee."

They sipped their coffee in silence. It was strong and black, just the way they both liked it. Finishing their coffee, they each put their cups aside as Jonas pushed a file across his desk to Nate.

"This is a hot one, Nate. Can you clear everything else off your plate?"

"Sure, if need be. What's so special about this case?"

"It involves the serving district attorney down in Eisenberg. Seems he's married but had a Mexican girlfriend across the river. She was also married and whenever her wandering spouse decided to come home, she'd give McKenzie – that's the guy's name, Edgar McKenzie – the cold shoulder. Well, I guess McKenzie got enough of it and solicited a jailbird to have a buddy of his kill the husband. The prisoner told the sheriff, the sheriff told the FBI. They wired the prisoner and got Edgar cold."

"So, what's so hot about this case? Sounds like a simple compulsory discipline case based on a criminal conviction."

"You'd think so but so far, he's beat the feds, who indicted him for perjury and for conspiracy to commit murder. The proceedings were dismissed on jurisdictional grounds. Next, a special prosecutor put him on trial in a state court for the crimes of solicitation and conspiracy to commit murder. His lawyers filed a motion to suppress the recordings because of entrapment. It was granted and the case was dismissed. Finally, the Prosecutors Coordinating Council filed suit to remove him from office."

"Excuse me, Jonas – what's that?"

"I had to look it up myself," said Jonas. "Seems last session of the legislator it created this state agency to police local elected prosecutors and to provide some minimal continuing education. May have been a good idea but as usual, the good ole boys were stingy with the money. All the appropriated funds paid for was one lawyer, as executive director and a secretary. The statute provides for a board, and again, I'm not real clear on this, but it apparently got organized and hired a former prosecutor. Anyway, this guy files suit to remove McKenzie from office. The case gets dismissed on a motion under the "prior term" doctrine since the acts complained of occurred before McKenzie's re-election. There were appeals but, in the end, the case was dismissed and so McKenzie and his lawyers are pretty full of themselves now."

"The case is hot because the area – not the local – media is raising hell. So is the local bar association and the grievance committee. The county is divided between those who think McKenzie should be in jail and those who, at least publicly, act like they believe he is the victim of a governmental conspiracy of some sort. The latter group seems to be in the majority and the more vocal. McKenzie as I understand it, is like the political godfather of Bayon County, so whether his support arises from fear or actual belief, again I don't know. But there you have it," Jonas concluded.

"Was it local politics or his lawyers that helped him skate?" asked Nate.

"A little of both, seems to me. But don't underestimate his legal team. I'm told that in the Valley, they're considered first rate. He's got Randy Owens, a criminal defense lawyer, and Jack Lewis, a civil trial attorney retained."

"Never heard of either," said Nate. "Are either the feds or the state thinking of further action?"

"That, again, is something I know nothing of. But I suppose it is a possibility. Why do you ask?

"Well," said Nate, "I was wondering if he thinks he'll have to take the 5th. Shorten the trial if he does."

Nate went to his office and after reviewing the file, discovered there was no copy of the transcribed recordings. He called the chairman of the grievance committee. No, he didn't have a copy. He borrowed the state prosecutor's copy but had to give it back and hadn't been allowed to make a copy. Nate then called the prosecutor. Yes, he had a copy but couldn't let go of it even to make a copy, he was still trying to decide what to do. The listed number for the prosecutor's council went unanswered. Nate called the FBI office in San Antonio. Yes, they had a copy but as the file was still active blah, blah. The attorney in the U.S. Attorney's Office in Brownsville that he spoke to said their file had gone into storage and he didn't know exactly where it was or how to reclaim the file even if it were located. *What the hell?* Thought Nate.

About that time, he got a call from the grievance committee chairman who asked if he'd located the transcript. Nate said he hadn't. Well try the 5th circuit, the chairman said. He thought he'd heard that the U.S. Attorney had filed an appeal contesting the finding of lack of jurisdiction. He understood that the appeal was unsuccessful, but the transcript surely was a part of the appellate record. Nate thanked him and called the clerk of court in New Orleans. The lady who answered would check and call him back. While he could work around it, surely once he filed suit the FBI agent witness would share the transcript. Without it he would have to just wing his pleadings based on the grievance committee's account. Not fatal but a pain nevertheless.

His angst disappeared when the lady in New Orleans called back, "Yes, there was a copy of the transcript in the file." If he wanted a certified copy, it would be eighty-seven dollars and fifty cents.

"Check's in the mail," Nate said.

After receiving and reviewing the transcript, Nate prepared and mailed to the District Clerk in Bayon County, the original disciplinary petition, requests for admissions, and interrogatories. Nate did not expect to gain anything by serving the latter two discovery requests but the manner in which McKenzie's attorneys responded or did not respond and the actions later of the trial court might reveal something of substance that could prove useful.

In due course, Nate received a general denial and, as he had expected, nothing but the customary objections to his discovery requests. He promptly prepared and mailed to Bayon County a motion to compel. He requested the clerk to obtain a setting and noted in his letter that any time between the hours of 1:30 p.m. and 4:30 p.m. would be greatly appreciated as the only direct flight from Austin arrived at 1:00 p.m. and departed at 6:00 p.m.

Several days later, he received a notice of setting for 10:00 a.m. ten days hence. *So, that's how it's going to be* he thought. Because of the mid-morning setting, he could not take the direct Southwest flight; instead he had to take the six o'clock a.m. flight from Austin, which went through Houston and then to the Valley, arriving at nine o'clock a.m. He rented a car and drove to Eisenberg. He arrived at the county courthouse about twenty minutes before the hour.

He found a parking place and hurried into the courthouse. The courthouse was a five-story steel, marble, and glass structure. It was a large rectangle, dun-colored, aspiring to be postmodern in style, but having small claim to style of any kind. Nate entered the first-floor double doors and took the elevator up to the third floor.

He was in his seat at the counsel table a few minutes before ten o'clock. He was alone. So, he waited; no one appeared. Finally after thirty minutes, Nate made his way to the district clerk's office. After waiting at the window for some time, he was able to attract the attention of one of the clerks.

In response to his inquiry she said, "Oh, I'm sorry, weren't you notified? The hearing has been reset for four this afternoon. Judge Canales had some kind of a conflict."

What kind of a conflict thought Nate? His courtroom is deserted. These bastards are playing me again. I'll probably miss my return flight and I didn't bring a change of clothes or anything with me. Shit! Guess I'll go get some lunch and go visit the Sheriff.

At 4:00 Nate was in the courtroom as were McKenzie and his attorneys. Nate went over to introduce himself and McKenzie and his attorneys got up and walked away. *Good God* thought Nate, *What kind of people are these?* He returned to his seat and watched the clock. At a little past 5:15 Judge Canales emerged and took his seat. Hector Canales, seemed to be fairly young, had dark skin was slight of build with close cropped black hair and steel spectacles, through which he was constantly squinting as though his prescription was outdated.

He called the case number and asked for announcements of ready. Both sides announced they were ready to proceed. Canales lifted a file from in front of him and with shaking hands gave a show of reviewing the contents. After a minute or two, he looked up and said, looking at Nate, “I’ve reviewed your motion and it’s denied.”

Nate was dumbfounded. “With all due respect your honor, you are not even going to give me a chance to present the grounds for my motion – no arguments? I’ve flown all the way from Austin, I’ve waited here all day long and now I have no opportunity to pursue my motion?”

Judge Canales, his voice cracking through several octaves, his face turning crimson rose partially out of his seat, pointed a finger at Nate and said, “One more word and I’ll hold you in contempt and have you thrown in jail. You do not question this court’s rulings!” With that he slid sideways from the bench and was out the door.

Nate, in stunned silence, looked around. McKenzie and his attorneys, with satisfied smirks on their faces were exiting the courtroom as fast as they could move without actually trotting.

Back in Austin after a miserable night and an early morning three-hour flight with a lay-over in Houston, Nate stopped at his house only long enough to shower, shave, and change clothes and check on Cat. Upon arriving at his office, he immediately called the chairman of the grievance committee in Bayon County.

After his recitation of his treatment of the previous day, he was surprised to hear a chuckle rather than words of support. “So, you’ve met our Hector, eh?”

“Yes, I have,” Nate said, “what’s going on with him – is it me or does he treat everyone that way, or is he just nuts?”

“You got it,” said the chairman, “he’s bat shit crazy.”

“What? How can that be tolerated?”

“His family has roots damn near back to Cortes. They are the major landowners in the Valley, in cattle, horses, and I don’t know how many farms raising vegetables and fruit. They also have a canning factory. Altogether they must have near a thousand employees – more at harvest time. Also, I guess I should have warned you, they are big supporters of McKenzie’s. As to Hector,” he continued, “we all just work around him. You donate to the clerk; she puts your case in another court. About all Hector gets are change of names, adoption, and uncontested cases of all kinds. To paraphrase Winston Churchill’s observation of Americans, Hector does the right thing when he has no alternative.”

“I’m going to recuse him,” promised Nate.

“Good luck with that.”

Having filed such a motion and being notified of the hearing thereon, Nate flew down and entered the courtroom. All the seats behind the rail were filled. Klieg lights blinded him as he surveyed the room. At least three television cameras and crews were visible in the rear. *Surreal was a gigantic understatement,* thought Nate as he took his seat. After about five minutes, much to Nate’s astonishment, Hector Canales strode to the bench and called the court to order.

He glared at Nate as Nate rose. “Your honor, I think there must be a mistake. I respectively suggest that under the rules of procedure, you cannot preside at your own removal proceeding," said Nate.

Canales, his face beginning to darken and a sliver of drool forming on his lower lip, in a voice approaching a shriek, said, "Don't you dare tell this court what the law is. But for your information, I recused myself days ago before you filed your motion and under the local rules, I have transferred this case to Joe Jackson."

"Well, if you have recused yourself, may I ask why I am here?"

"You are here to answer my questions."

"Your Honor, I am sorry, but you have no jurisdiction any more to do anything."

"This is the last time I am going to warn you about trying to tell this court what it can and cannot do. I am on the verge of having you thrown in jail."

"With respect, Judge, you know you can't do that. I'm entitled to a hearing before another judge before I can be held in contempt."

Ignoring Nate's reply, Canales proceeded, "Are you deliberately being contemptuous of this court?"

"Your honor, I am doing my best to hide it," Nate replied so softly that only those just behind the rail heard. Even so there was a small peal of laughter which Canales quickly gaveled to silence.

"What did you say?" Canales demanded in a voice now almost a screech.

"Nothing your honor," answered Nate.

"I'm warning you, I'm getting real tired of your attitude mister. Now tell me are you going to amend your petition?"

What the hell does he care and what's the big deal, thought Nate. He replied, "Your Honor, as you know, I have freedom to amend my pleadings without leave of court up to seven days before trial. I honestly have not even thought about it at this time."

Canales, his face now almost purple, with foam literally forming on his lips, shouted at Nate, "You will answer my question!"

Nate, taken aback by this spectacle, could only manage a muffled reply, "Your Honor, I have answered your question the best I could."

Canales, as though struck in the chest, slumped backward into his chair. He gazed slowly around the courtroom as though seeking allies. Apparently finding no assistance, he took hold of his gavel, brought it down with a whack and in a timorous voice announced the court was adjourned. He then, more or less, staggered from the bench. *Nate remained standing, staring incredulously at the* retreating black robed figure. *I've never ever seen anything like that, he thought to himself.* Arousing himself, he avoided the reporters and made it back to the airport and back to Austin.

Next day he called the chairman of the grievance committee, the committee being his client, and wasn't surprised to hear the chairman had heard of the previous day's debacle. "I hear you've now experienced Valley justice," he said.

"What a crazy son-of-a-bitch," said Nate. "I really thought he was going to have the sheriff's deputies haul me off to jail. And what the hell was going on with the T.V. cameras and reporters? Man, I remember what you said but I still have a hard time accepting that guy as a judge."

"On the bright side, I've at least got a new judge, even though I have questions about the legality of his appointment. After the hearing, I went to the clerk's office and asked to see the order recusing Canales and appointing Jackson. I wanted to see the date it was signed. Guess what? The clerk couldn't find it."

"That stuff with the T.V. was off the map even for Canales. I have no idea what all that was for. As for the missing order, I'm not surprised. McKenzie has the whole courthouse beholden to him. As for as your bright side, I hate to tell you, but it ain't very bright. Jack Lewis, McKenzie's lead attorney was Judge Jackson's campaign manager when Jackson ran for re-election last year."

"There's just no end to this shit, is there? Well, screw them. I'm going to notice McKenzie for a deposition, commit him to taking the 5th on the record, lock him in, and then set this damn case for trial. I'm tired of getting jacked around," said Nate.

Prior to McKenzie's scheduled deposition, Nate flew back down to the Valley and met with his witnesses. He was impressed with Tom Hatch, the FBI agent who appeared to be extremely competent and well prepared. Tony, Guzman, and even Noe and Mia would be fine. The day arrived for McKenzie's deposition. Nate caught the noon direct flight from Austin, rented a car upon arrival and drove to the offices of Lewis, Herrera and Lane, P.C., in Eisenberg. The office was a one-story stone building on a corner lot two blocks south of the courthouse.

As Nate entered the reception area, he noticed a young and attractive Mexican woman. He assumed she was the court reporter and he and she exchanged introductions. She gave only her first name, Leticia. Next Nate introduced himself to the receptionist who asked him to take a seat and she would check with Mr. Lewis.

She was gone for about ten minutes, and when she returned, she asked Nate and the reporter to follow her. She opened a door to the left which led to a large, paneled room. A large walnut table occupied the center, dark leather armchairs were arranged around the table, four to a side and one at each end. There was a large whiteboard on the right-hand wall and a television set on a wheeled cart in the corner. Three large windows filled the street side wall and provided light in spite of the partially closed curtains.

Nate and the reporter took their seats, no coffee or water was offered. The young lady who had shown them in left without a word. So, they sat. After thirty minutes, Nate was ready to have the reporter do a certificate of non-appearance when, without warning, the door at the opposite end of the room opened. In stalked Edgar McKenzie and Jack Lewis, neither making eye contact with either Nate or the reporter. Lewis seated himself at the head of the table with McKenzie to his left. Nate arose and extended his hand to Lewis.

Lewis ignored it and announced in a gruff voice, “We’re ready.”

Nate and the reporter had to move closer to the two seated figures. The reporter in a timorous voice asked Edgar to raise his hand while she recited the oath.

After first looking to Lewis, McKenzie raised his hand and said, “I do.” Nate’s first question was to ask the witness if his name was Edgar McKenzie. McKenzie glared at him and then said, “On the advice of counsel I will not answer, and I take advantage of the Fifth Amendment to the U.S. Constitution.”

"That's ridiculous," said Nate. "How can giving your name incriminate you?"

Lewis slapped the table and began to rise from his chair. "Don't you talk to my client. Talk to me."

"Your client is a witness pursuant to due notice and under oath, I have every right to question him."

"Then get on with it," said Lewis in a surly voice.

Nate started to respond, thought better of it, and asked McKenzie. "You are the serving district attorney of Bayon County?"

McKenzie, in a monotone replied he was taking the Fifth Amendment.

Nate asked if McKenzie was a member of the State Bar of Texas.

Same answer.

Nate asked if McKenzie knew Manual Guzman.

Same answer.

Looking to Lewis, Nate said, "Look if your client is going to take the Fifth Amendment to every question I ask, how about we save some time and so stipulate on the record?"

Without looking at Nate, Lewis replied in the same tone of voice, "We don't stipulate to anything. Ask your questions."

So, for the next hour and twenty minutes, Nate asked his questions and received the same response.

Finally, he said, "Pass the witness."

Whereupon Lewis and McKenzie rose from their chairs and without a word went back through the door through which they had entered.

The hostility in the air was palpable even without the presence of the two men. It lingered so heavily that that the reporter's hands shook as she was collecting her equipment. There might even have been a tear in her eye.

Nate said very sincerely, "look, I'm so sorry, I had no way of knowing it would be this unpleasant."

"It's not your fault, but thanks. I'll get you a copy by the end of the week." Nate opened the doors for her, and they left without speaking.

Nate felt guilty but he knew this fiasco had not been his fault. He knew too that this was the first of many more. He drove back to the airport, turned in his car, and waited at the bar until his six o'clock direct flight back to Austin. He had a couple of margaritas while he sat and brooded over the events at the Lewis office. *What did they think they gained by being such assholes? Was Lewis playing badass for his client? Surely, he wasn't like that all the time. Finally, Nate said to himself, hell with it. I don't know why I'm so pissed off. I got what I wanted. I only filled the paper discovery and the deposition notice to check out McKenzie's lawyers and maybe the judge. Boy, I got that in spades. New guy can be as bad as the last one. They'll raise hell and file motions, but I've got the bastard nailed to the fifth. He's dead meat no matter what he and his attorneys do.* With that Nate boarded his flight, found a seat and took a nap.

Chapter 7 – Courtship of Jen

In the meanwhile, Nate had pursued Jen, not without her encouragement. Weekend afternoons at Barton Creek, swimming in the cold refreshing aquifer fed waters, picnics on the sloping lawn, dancing at Emos, sausages, sauerkraut, and beer at Schultz's Garden, the best that Austin had to offer and not to short Willie Nelson at Armadillo World Headquarters and the Broken Spoke.

It was one night after their date at the Broken Spoke that momentarily threatened their romance. Their relationship, in the normal progression, had moved from "good nights," to chaste kisses, to passionate embraces at Jen's door. This night she invited Nate in for coffee. They both had drank more than usual. As Jen stood at the counter making coffee, she turned to Nate with a look he had never seen, equal parts longing and apprehension.

Nate took her in his arms and kissed her. She returned the kiss with unusual fervor. She stiffened as she felt Nate's arousal and then thrust herself into him. Their tongues dueled for purchase. Nate lifted her and carried her to her bedroom. In a frenzy clothes were shed and scattered as they fell upon her bed. Just before he entered her, Jen whispered "I've never ..." "Should I stop?" gasped Nate. In response Jen's grip around his neck tightened and she pulled him into her.

Nate awoke at sunrise. The first feeble rays of dawn were creeping in between the blinds. Nate had decided it was best to leave, he didn't want Jen to be embarrassed. Jen was lying on her side, facing away from him with the sheet partly above her hips. As he admired her firm body and long tan legs, he almost lost his resolve.

With a force of will, he silently rolled from the bed, gathered his clothes, and after donning them hurriedly left the apartment.

At noon, Nate drove over to the clinic. He didn't call first since he was not sure of Jen's reaction. After asking for her at the desk, he sat and waited with some trepidation. Jen appeared flashing a smile, but he sensed some reticence in her attitude.

Jen led him through a side door into a small, enclosed courtyard. They seated themselves on a bench and Jen spoke first.

"I didn't expect to see you," she said. "I mean, you were gone when I woke up, so I wasn't sure, you know, what was going on."

"Yeah, I know, I just thought, I mean, I didn't know how you'd feel, me still being there."

"Well, when you weren't there, I thought maybe you'd gotten what you wanted and you know ..."

"Jen, no, no, how can you think that? Maybe, I made a mistake, but I love you and I want to marry you."

"You want to make an honest woman of me?"

"Jen, please, what happened last night, happened. That has nothing to do with my feelings – no, that's not right, last night made me love you more. I've loved you since the first time I saw you. Please say you'll marry me."

"No," said Jen.

"What?" said Nate. "I thought ... I mean we seemed to be so good together. I can't believe one night would change everything – I'm so sorry, I'll do anything to make it up to you. At least say you'll think about it."

"Nate, I'm not blaming you. I'm a full-grown woman and I played an equal part last night. In fact, if I'm honest I would have to say that I never felt so completely fulfilled and safe. I want to say I love you and that I'll marry you but, please try to understand, there's some little doubt in the back of my mind. If this makes you angry and you decide you never want to see me again, I guess I can understand, that's not what I want, but I guess it's up to you."

I love you, thought Nate, probably the most hackneyed phrase in the English language, but yet what other words can convey such a grand emotion? Simple yet so complex.

"Jen, I know you can't possibly believe all I wanted was a one-night stand. I'm not ashamed of last night. In fact, it was wonderful. I thought it was a fulfillment of our love. But if you want me to prove how I feel about you, I'm more than willing."

So, they continued dating in the waning days of summer. Fall came and Jen left for College Station to resume her studies. Nate visited on weekends and their relationship remained as warm and close as ever. The first weekend or two Nate stayed in a motel. Then motel rooms became impossible to secure because of football game crowds. So, they agreed that when he was able to visit, Nate would sleep on the couch in Jen's front room.

Chapter 8 – Welcome to Bayon County

Early on the Sunday morning before the trial was to begin, Nate packed his bags, arranged for his landlord's married daughter, who lived two doors down, to check on Cat, called Jen, who wished him "good luck," got into his car and headed out of Austin on I-35 South. At New Braunfels, he turned onto State Highway 6 to Boerne and then to Comfort.

He had been here many times before to stand silently and view the obelisk commemorating the massacre of thirty-seven German Americans by Confederate forces and militia. Somehow these visits tightened his sense of duty and resolve. These men had died for their principles. They had not retreated from their oaths. Neither could he. These men had been slaughtered because they sought to evade conscription into the southern army, an army waging war against the government they had sworn loyalty to. A government that offered freedom from the oppressive rule of their fatherland.

No battle had been fought here. The bodies that rested in this graveyard had been removed from the Neches River site of the one sided battle. Why this place was so meaningful to him, Nate did not understand. After all, none of his forebears lay here.

Even stranger, his great-grandfather had indeed fought for the Confederacy during the Civil War. Not of his free will, however, he fought. His great-grandfather opposed slavery and had done all he could to avoid taking sides in the struggle. Ever since his arrival in Texas in 1857, all he had ever wanted was to be left alone to work his land. His plan was frustrated when on a business trip to Corinth, Mississippi, in 1861, he was seized and conscripted into Company D, 22nd Regiment, Mississippi

Infantry, Confederate States Army. The 22nd participated in more than forty various types of engagements. Its final one, insofar as Nate's great-grandfather was concerned, was the battle of Champion's Hill.

At that time, the 22nd was a part of Featherston's Brigade, Loring's Division, Stewart's Corps, Army of Tennessee commanded by Lt. General Pemberton. Pemberton's ill-advised and insubordinate refusal to link up with Joseph Johnson's army led to a series of losing battles culminating in his surrender of Vicksburg. Champion's Hill was just outside Vicksburg and the battle hardly slowed Grant in his inexorable campaign to destroy the Confederate strong point on the Mississippi River.

Nate's great-grandfather was captured during the battle and imprisoned in notorious Fort Delaware. Rather than face sure death by disease or starvation, he, like many others, agreed to parole and enlistment in the United States Army under an agreement to be stationed in the western United States. Their duty was to garrison various forts to protect settlers from Indian raids.

It was ironic, Nate mused, that four generations of his family had, in fact, been warriors, albeit reluctant ones, and all had served with star crossed formations. His grandfather, in World War One, who had his left arm shattered by German machine gun bullets during the Meuse-Argonne offensive, for the rest of his life cursed Pershing and other AEF senior commanders for their outmoded tactics of reliance on infantry armed with rifles and bayonets to win battles in the face of murderous artillery and machine gun fire. A stubborn refusal to relinquish outstated linear formations and frontal assaults, even as their allies implored them to adopt their hard learned tactics, caused thousands and thousands of unnecessary doughboy deaths and wounds. This was especially true of the 35th Division, a National Guard unit made up mostly of guardsmen from Missouri and Kansas to which his grandfather had been assigned as a replacement.

His grandfather had honorably served his country in spite of the anti-German sentiments then being spread across the nation. Though these existed prior to Wilson's unconstitutional sedition laws, which served to incarcerate hundreds of innocent German immigrants and to harass thousands more for simply exercising their First Amendment rights, these laws served to justify and intensify such attitudes.

Nate's father was drafted in WWII and posted to the 106th infantry division. It was an untested division assigned to what was considered a quiet sector of the front in the Ardennes region of Belgium, on December 12, 1944. It was responsible for a twenty-one-mile section in a salient which jutted deeply into German lines. The division had been in place for only four days when the quiet of the cold, fog shrouded dawn was violently shattered by German panzers, supported by infantry, which burst suddenly upon the startled Americans.

In the mid-December freezing cold and still near dark dawn, the panzers raced through the fir trees and barbed-wire and over the frozen snow-covered ground crushing foxholes, and the men inside, spitting death in every direction. The division taken utterly by surprise was unable to offer any organized resistance. Here and there officers and NCO's attempted to form defensive positions, but they were swept aside by the onslaught. Soon the survivors just ran for their lives.

Nate's father was swept along by the retreating tide. He wandered alone over the frozen unfamiliar terrain for three days and nights. He had no food and ate snow to lessen his thirst as he played cat and mouse with German patrols. Finally, half dead, he stumbled into American lines. He lost two toes to frost bite.

Allied intelligence had totally failed to detect the enemy buildup. Incompetence, indolence, simply the fog of war, whatever, wondered Nate, this sort of thing seemed to play a tragic role in his family's history. He returned to his car and retraced his route through Boerne and then he turned south at San Antonio and then onto US 281 South to Eisenberg.

The highway was wide and straight, and the vintage BMW ate up the miles. The countryside was mostly sun burned grass lands, the victim of the Texas August sun. Now and again small herds of cattle clustered together in the sparse shade of mesquite trees and small wooded areas. The hot wind threatened to sear the skin as it blew through the windows. The temperature was in the high nineties, and one could imagine the asphalt was nearing its melting point.

Nate drove through isolated settlements, which hardly deserved the sobriquet of "town." Toward evening he reached his destination and, as he drove into the courthouse square, he was met face on with a banner stretched across the street. It proudly proclaimed, "Edgar McKenzie Appreciation Day."

The trash barrels on the square were overflowing with paper cups and plates. Small groups of people, mostly men, clustered here and there. The caterers were packing their equipment. Nate's first thought was *it must have been some bash. His next thought was, what in the hell have I gotten into?*

He drove until he found his motel. After checking in and bringing his suitcase into his room, he called the Sheriff and arranged to meet him for breakfast. The Sheriff volunteered that he had kept tabs on the local witnesses, and they were all available. His next call was to Hatch in San Antonio. The FBI agent was prepped and ready on standby. Being thus reassured, Nate went to dinner.

When he returned to his room and unlocked his door, he found his room in disarray. The bed covers were on the floor, a chair had been tipped over and the clothes he had carefully either hung in the closet or placed in the bureau drawers were scattered about the room. Nate was furious as he stormed to the motel office. He slammed the door shut as he entered apparently waking the elderly Mexican lady at the desk.

"Who did you give my room key to?" he demanded. The small-wrinkled face stared back at him uncomprehending. "My door was locked when I left and locked when I returned. So, whoever trashed my room had to have a key." "I saw no one," the tiny person replied. Her eyes by now were wide open and large and she seemed to tense herself to repel an attack.

"Have you been at this desk for the last two hours?" Nate demanded. The gray head slowly nodded up and down. "Is there more than one key to each room?" The head nodded again. "My room is 12A, do you have the other key?" The elderly lady busied herself in the drawer in front of her and finally produced a key. She smiled, or at least that was what Nate observed she was attempting – her expression had hardly changed.

Realizing there was little to be gained in prolonging this one-sided conversation, Nate returned to his room. There he debated with himself whether or not to call the police. He decided against it. He felt no threat of physical harm. He decided the break-in itself was less an attempt to discover any confidential information than it was a message. Not unlike the bar-b-que and banner. Nothing had been taken, so point of fact, a call to the police would be pointless anyway. Nate took a shower and went to bed.

Early the next morning, he met the Sheriff for breakfast in the motel coffee shop. They each ordered and while waiting for their food, Nate mentioned the courthouse square celebration and the rifling of his room. After being told nothing had been taken because Nate had kept his court files locked safely in the trunk of his car, the sheriff stated the obvious, that there was little he could do. But as to the other matter, he handed Nate a wrinkled piece of paper containing five or six names. The Sheriff explained he had a plain-clothes deputy attend McKenzie's bar-b-que and checked off a list of prospective jurors he had obtained from the district clerk. The names on the marked paper were the ones the deputy recognized as belonging on the venue. Nate thanked him as their food arrived.

The Sheriff arose and walked out onto the back patio area. He returned with a handful of chiltepin peppers. He offered some to Nate before dropping those in his hand onto his eggs.

"Bird peppers they're called by the locals," he said. "Nice and hot," as he wiped his hand on his napkin. "I'm crazy about them, I put them on everything – gives a lotta taste. Anytime I see any, I always grab them, wild ones taste better than the ones they sell at the nursery."

After breakfast, Nate and Sheriff Catalon drove to the courthouse in separate cars. They parked and walked up the front steps to find a deputy sheriff standing in front of the doors. The Sheriff seemed not only surprised to find the deputy there but somewhat put out at what appeared to be an afront to his authority.

Testily, he asked, “Earnesto, what the hell’s going on?”

“The dispatch tried to reach you, but your radio was off,” Earnesto replied. “So, I was sent over here, there was some kinda bomb threat. The doors have been locked and the county judge told me to keep everybody away.”

“So, is anybody checking things out?” asked Catalon.

“Sheriff, there’s nobody in there and right now no one’s doing anything. I understand the FBI in San Antonio has been called and they are sending a bomb squad. Same with Kingsland AFB cause as you know the local agencies don’t have the expertise to deal with something like this. It will take a while for either to get here, so all I can tell you is everyone is just waiting.”

“I guess there’ll be no court today,” said the Sheriff. “Have you heard how the threat was made?”

“Yes, sir,” Earnesto replied. “It was an anonymous telephone call to the courthouse switchboard this morning right at eight o’clock. The operator said it sounded like the caller was in a well, or something”

“Obviously disguised,” said Catalon. “No way then to tell who it was.”

Nate returned to his motel after the Sheriff promised to call him when the threat had been resolved. The call came at four o’clock. No bomb, no clues as to the source of the call. Given the time, Nate broke out his files and briefly reviewed his trial notes. Although his trial was not a cause of major concern, the custom of going through the file was a reassuring routine.

So, too, as always, he recalled the two "do-nots" of a trial lawyer; never ask a question you do not know the answer to and never ask that one question too many. Also came the memory of an apocryphal tale out of East Texas that members of the bar had quoted for years as highlighting both cautions.

It seems a prominent Gulf Coast attorney, a senior partner in a large defense firm, was defending an intersection collision case. The plaintiff's star witness was an elderly black gentleman who had been sitting in a rocking chair on the front porch of a black funeral home. He swore he had seen the plaintiff's car in the intersection when the defendant's car ran a stop sign striking the plaintiff's car and injuring him. The witness appeared to have had cataract surgery because he was wearing glasses whose lenses looked like the bottom of a coke bottle.

The senior attorney could hardly wait to get to the witness. His first several questions flew within minutes of the plaintiff's counsel passing the witness. After those several questions, designed mainly to get the attention of the witness, the attorney began his thrust to the jugular.

"Can you look at the rear of the courtroom and tell me what time is on the clock?"

The witness squinted his eyes and moved around in his seat and after several minutes, he replied, "No, suh I can't make it out."

The attorney next turned to the calendar over the jury box. Bancroft and Whitney, a law book company, for many years mailed huge calendars, perhaps thirty by forty-two inches to all its subscribers. Those mailed to small county law libraries inevitably ended up in a courtroom, usually over the jury box. The calendar had the name of the publisher in large black capital letters, then a historical print and below that a pad of the months of the year.

"Can you look at the calendar over the jury box and read me the name in the big black letters?"

Again, the witness squinted, he rubbed his eyes, moved around a little in his seat and finally said, "Sorry suh, I can't exactly make it out."

"Well, tell me, just how far can you see?"

The witness thought a moment, rubbed his chin and replied, "Well suh, I can see the moon and stars, how far is that?" The courtroom, of course, broke out in laughter. All the attorney could do was to say weakly, "Pass the witness."

Nate smiled to himself and went to take a shower.

Chapter 9 – The Trial

Tuesday morning, court began on time with Judge Jackson presiding. Jackson was of medium height with close cropped gray hair, an above average waistline and heavy black plastic frame glasses which he now wore pushed to the top of his forehead. Voir dire of the prospective jurors proceeded slowly. Both sides subjected the panel members to a barrage of questions to the increasing irritation of Judge Jackson.

Finally, Jackson called the attorneys up to the bench. "Now look, I've given both sides a lot of leeway here, but I think this business can be shortened. I want the *voir dire* finished before the noon recess. The jury will be seated, and the trial will start after lunch with opening statements. Do I make myself clear?"

"Yes sir," said both attorneys with one voice.

By two o'clock, the lunch hour having been moved up, the panel was seated. Each side was allowed one hour for its opening statement. The Plaintiff opened.

Before standing, Nate surveyed the courtroom. His eyes rested for a moment upon a lady he had been informed was Julia McKenzie. She sat behind the rail directly to the rear of her husband. She wore an expensive yet simple suit. Her hair, mostly gray with patches of brown, hung straight to her shoulders. Her angular face, devoid of makeup, faced forward unmoving, the only movement came from her eyes which constantly traversed the area in front of the rail as though she sensed danger. She appeared to be small in stature, not slim, but not yet succumbing to the additional weight all too often ushered in by later years. *Late fifties or early sixties*, thought

Nate, *probably works out. Does not look as though she is enjoying herself.*

As he continued his brief survey of the courtroom, his eyes rested upon a trim female figure in the last row. *Mia, he thought, well, she's here. I wonder if McKenzie's lawyers will let her stay in the audience until I call her to testify.*

Then Nate took his place before the jury and in a well-organized and sincere manner explained who he was, what the proceeding was about and what he expected to prove. He avoided any mention of the tapes or the Fifth Amendment but, instead, requested the jury to pay attention to the witnesses and the evidence.

He concluded by saying, "A license to practice law is a privilege, granted on condition that the licensee will honor his oath. That oath binds such persons to obey the laws and Constitution. Whoever violates that oath forfeits his right to practice law. How much more grievous is it when a lawyer sworn to enforce the law violates that oath as well. Ladies and gentlemen, you will hear how Edgar McKenzie violated his oath and brought shame and discredit upon his profession and his elected office." The defense deferred its opening.

Court began the next morning with the defense, as expected, urging its motions to suppress the recordings and to prohibit the plaintiff from commenting on the defendant's election to invoke the Fifth Amendment. Judge Jackson quickly denied both motions as premature with leave to present them at the appropriate time. Both motions would be considered in camera and Nate was ordered by the court to advise the court in advance of when he intended to introduce the tapes or to comment on McKenzie's assertion of his Fifth Amendment rights.

Nate called Guzman as his first witness and his direct testimony continued until noon. After the lunch break, Nate noticed two sheriff's deputies at the courtroom door. As he entered the courtroom, the bailiff summoned the attorneys to the chambers of Judge Jackson.

As the attorneys seated themselves in front of his desk, he greeted them severely, "I want to know who's behind the shit that's going on and I want it stopped!" When the attorneys showed no signs of comprehension, he continued, "During the noon hour a threat was made against Mr. Keller's life by another damn anonymous telephone call." Looking directly at Lewis and Owens, Jackson continued, his face by now crimson, "A bomb threat and now this – I won't have it, do you understand me?"

Indignantly Jack Lewis spoke up, "Judge you're looking at Randy and me, but I swear, neither of us know anything about this stuff."

"I ain't accusing anybody of anything," said Judge Jackson, "but it don't make no sense that Keller would threaten his own life. I'm calling Austin for Rangers. In the meanwhile, the sheriff will provide protection for Mr. Keller. Court will be recessed until tomorrow morning. Now all of you get the hell outta my office."

Nate, with a sheriff's car following him to his motel and then to dinner, was more puzzled than concerned. Was McKenzie behind this? Or was it some of his more ardent supporters? In either case these threats were doomed to failure. The case would proceed eventually with or without Nate. Nate finally decided that McKenzie surely recognized the inevitability of the proceeding and therefore was not personally involved. While this decision had no effect upon the threats themselves, it enabled Nate to turn his mind back to the trial. After reviewing his notes, Nate pulled his motel curtain to one side and saw a sheriff's patrol car in the parking lot. The light was too dim to tell whether or not there was anyone in the vehicle. Nate shrugged and went to bed.

Court began the next morning with a Texas Ranger at the courtroom entrance and one inside the rear of the courtroom.

Nate proceeded with the testimony of Guzman who made a good witness with a straightforward accounting of his interaction with McKenzie, the recording, etc. He stayed on course in spite of the constant interruptions by the defense in raising one baseless objection after the other in the vain hope, apparently, that one might be sustained. Surprisingly, many were after heated arguments before the bench. Nate was thrown off his rhythm but managed to rephrase his questions so that eventually he was able to elicit the testimony he sought. Finally, the day ended.

As Nate walked out the door, he spoke to the Ranger. "There's only two of you, how are you going to guard me twenty-four-seven?"

"Sir," said the Ranger, "our orders are to guard the courtroom only."

"Oh," said Nate. "The powers that be aren't concerned whether I get killed or not, they just don't want to mess up the courtroom. Is that it?"

"Something like that, I guess."

Being thus reassured, Nate went to dinner, then to his motel and then to bed.

The trial dragged slowly on through five weeks. The courtroom audience changed but Mrs. McKenzie was always there in her usual place wearing the same stoic expression but perhaps, by now, a bit more wearied. The going had been frustrating, but Nate, as he said, took a bite and hung on and was satisfied with the state of his record. After laying the predicate for admission of the recordings by the FBI agent Hatch, he now moved for their admission.

Judge Jackson summoned the attorneys, together with FBI agent Hatch and the court reporter to his chambers after dismissing the jury for the rest of the day.

As soon as they were all seated, Lewis and Owens began their objections. Judge Jackson, who appeared to be curious about the contents of the recordings, let them talk for a while but finally announced he would take their objections under advisement and would rule after he heard the tapes. As the recordings began to roll and McKenzie 's peculiar voice echoed around the small office, Judge Jackson appeared to wilt.

He finally said, "That rips it," and laid his head down on his desk. After an uncomfortable pause, he finally raised his head saying," God damn that's Edgar's voice you all know it and I know it. The tapes are coming in."

Lewis and Owens were now practically shouting their objections. Judge Jackson arose from his seat, color draining from his face. His body sagging as he said in a low strained voice, "Objections noted, court will commence at eight tomorrow morning. You are all excused."

The next morning, FBI agent Hatch played the tapes. Minutes into the recording Mrs. McKenzie dabbing at her eyes hurriedly arose and left the courtroom. McKenzie his face drained of color, stared fixedly ahead. There was absolute silence in the room except for an occasional gasp as McKenzie's voice filled the room outlining the plot. A few of the onlookers also left their seats. The tapes played out and yet no one spoke or moved as though transfixed.

Finally, it was Nate's voice that dispelled the near hypnotic spell, "Pass the witness."

"No questions."

"Call your next witness," said Judge Jackson

Nate called McKenzie as his last witness under the adverse party rule. He had been saved for last because Nate wanted the jury to hear his voice soon after hearing the tapes and, even though he would not testify, Nate wanted him to take the Fifth Amendment, so he could comment on his refusal to testify. McKenzie took the stand and indeed invoked his rights under the Constitution not to give evidence against himself. After six or seven questions, Nate assumed his point was made and he passed the witness. The defense declined to question. Nate rested his case.

Lewis and Owens split the opening argument for the defense. Each was a version of the other. Neither was full spirited. Nate sensed that the attorneys were now simply playing their roles, apparently disheartened by the recordings. The defense's case consisted of four-character witnesses who swore McKenzie's character for truthfulness and honesty was good. Nate did not cross, and the defense rested.

Judge Jackson excused the jury and he and the attorneys once again gathered in his chambers to prepare the jury charge. All objections by the defense team were now summarily denied by Judge Jackson, who had now become Nate's ally, contrary to his earlier antagonism.

The next morning, Judge Jackson read the charge and the jury instructions to the jury, and it was then time for closing arguments. In his opening argument, Nate reviewed with the jury his remarks in his opening statement and pointed out the evidence that he believed supported them. He then sat down after going through the seventeen special issues in the jury charge and suggesting they should all be answered “yes” based upon the evidence.

Lewis and Owens had evidently availed themselves of some Dutch courage during the noon recess. Both of their faces were flushed. As Lewis began his argument he paused after only a few words and looked around the courtroom as though seeking to find something he had misplaced, and finally continued in an uncertain voice. He pointed to the testimony of the character witnesses and urged the jury not to hold McKenzie’s failure to testify against him as that was his constitutional right, a right hundreds of young men from the Valley had died to protect, etc., etc.

Owens, when it was his turn, staggered as he got up from his chair. In his deep voice, now somewhat slurred, he called upon the jury not to sully the reputation of a great Texan crime fighter and a great American.

The rest of his argument will never be known as he went to the flag stand to the left of the bench and wrapped the American flag around him as if it were a cloak. Then he and the flagpole slowly toppled to the floor. He lay there unmoving the flag covering him.

The stunned silence was broken by a few hesitant chuckles which soon became a full-fledged uproar as Jackson, himself fighting back a smile, pounded his gavel for order. The bailiff and Lewis helped Owens to his seat. He sat there uncomprehendingly looking neither right nor left.

Judge Jackson dryly announced, "I assume that the defense has now concluded its argument, Mr. Keller, you have the last argument."

Nate knew having a good case did not guarantee a win. The jury had to be persuaded. It was not about the law or procedure, certainly not about justice or even right or wrong, often times it wasn't even about facts. Because the only facts that mattered were whatever the jury chose to believe to be the facts. What it took in almost all cases was to find that one thing, that weakness, that inconsistency, that miscalculation, that misrepresentation, that secret, perhaps even that bit of darkness that your opponent did not want known. When you found it, you grabbed it, you polished it, you honed it, you made it your own and then at the optimum time, like an avenging angel, you laid the lie, the inconsistency, the stupidity, the falseness bare before the twelve.

In this case, there were no secrets anymore, but that didn't mean there was nothing to exploit. Just the opposite and Nate had the final argument. He normally did not get personal in a trial but this one was different. Edgar's defense team, with his apparent approval, had made it personal. It was time for pay back.

Nate now began to deliver body blows to the defense. "What kind of a man who claims to be an outstanding Texan and American plots to murder another human being? For what? Sheer jealousy? How noble is that? Is that a great Texan and American? I know none of you believe that. There can't be any doubt of his guilt – he wouldn't even take the stand and deny it. He hid behind the Constitution, well, that may be his right, and I don't deny him that, but it's our right to believe that if he were truly innocent, he would have taken the stand, looked you in the eye, and told you the charges were baseless. The truth is, he couldn't do that, you heard him on the tapes, and so he hid behind the Constitution. I tell you now that because he did so, you can infer his guilt."

Both Lewis and Owens were shouting their objections. The court instructed the jury to disregard the last remark. It didn't matter, of course, the jury had heard it already.

Barely missing a beat, Nate took up a transcript of the recordings. "You know," he said, "The court told you that what the lawyers said was not evidence. That doesn't mean that if your recollection is the same as mine, you should not consider it. I am going to read to you the Defendant's words out of his own mouth as I have written them down." Nate then read from the transcript and ended with, "'You know, it's too bad, but what the hell, he was a no-good little sumbitch anyway.' Ladies and gentlemen of the jury, are those the words of a great American and great Texan? I think not and I don't believe you think so either. This man does not deserve to have a license to practice law. The evidence in this case compels you to answer every issue 'yes.'"

The jury deliberated thirty-seven minutes. All issues were answered "yes." Jackson accepted the verdict, set the punishment phase of the trial for the following Monday, gave the jurors their instructions and recessed the trial.

Hatch and the Sheriff came over to congratulate Nate, as did most members of the grievance committee who, until now, had been noticeably absent from the courtroom during the trial, but who now appeared as if by some conjuror's trick. Like clients in general, some offered praise, others were more restrained. They, after all, had had the courage to vote out the complaint and had handed Nate an easy case. All he had had to do was not screw it up. Therefore, if applause was due, it was owed to them.

Lawyers, thought Nate, *were just as ungrateful as other clients. Oh, well, he thought, I didn't do this for pats on the back.* He proceeded to inform the grievance committee members to be present Monday as they would be called to testify as to the appropriate sanction. Whereupon even the most effusive members became less so.

Disengaging himself, Nate returned to his motel. He called Jen who eagerly responded to his inquiry. He hurriedly packed an overnight bag and hurried to his BMW. The long drive from the Valley to College Station had left Nate's body stiff. The exhaustion wrought by the past six weeks of contentious trial, together with the nightly sessions of preparation for the next day, added to these so that he felt as though he had lost control of his body. He parked and almost staggered to Jen's apartment door.

The hour was late when he knocked on her door. Jen had already bathed and was dressed in a robe and pajamas when she opened the door. Her sweet and tender kiss, accompanied as it was with the faint scent of lilacs and the warm glow of her skin momentarily chased away Nate's fatigue.

He declined her offer of food but accepted a Lone Star. He had no sooner sat down and taken a sip of his beer when his eyelids began to flutter, and his chin dipped to his chest. It was obvious to Jen the conversation was destined to be one-sided. She made up the couch, kissed Nate goodnight and retreated to her bedroom. Nate haltingly pulled off his shoes and clothes and allowed his body to fold itself onto the couch. Some hours later Nate became dimly aware of a sweet flow of breath accompanied by a tender caressing of his hair and then a butterfly kiss upon his lips.

From far away he heard, “Nate are you awake?”

Struggling to free himself from the embrace of his unconsciousness, Nate was barely able to utter, “Just about.”

Unfazed Jen continued, “Do you remember what you asked me twelve weeks ago?”

Nate’s awareness and memory were by now returning and he was able to ask, “the one you wanted to think about?”

“The answer is ‘yes,’ if you still want me.”

Nate was now fully awake, his senses so filled with emotion he was unable to speak. Jen’s face was mere inches from his as she knelt by his side. The window blinds permitted shafts of moonlight to filter through and these played upon her face bequeathing an ethereal quality to it. Breathing became a temporary concern for Nate. *I’ve never seen anything so beautiful*, he thought. By a force of will, he gathered himself sufficiently to say, “Of course I still want you – I always will.”

He attempted to rise from the couch and could see in the dappled light the shadowy outline of Jen’s body. She did not appear to be wearing any clothing. Jen’s lips pressed him backward onto the sofa. She shifted her head slightly and whispered into his ear, “Do you think there is room on the couch for both of us?” Without waiting for a reply, in one lithe movement her body glided onto his.

Practically giddy by the events of the weekend, thrilled but at the same time wary, that so much pure happiness could come to him, Nate, on late Sunday afternoon, returned to his motel room in Eisenberg. Now to be more lonely than before.

Chapter 10 – Back to Bayon County

The sanctions proceedings continued for two weeks but presented no surprises. As everyone recognized, they were anticlimactic but since they were desired by Judge Jackson for political cover, all the participants played their roles. At the conclusion, Jackson found that Edgar was guilty of professional misconduct and entered a judgment of disbarment and demanded McKenzie's law license and State Bar card. Following the announcement of the judgment, there was the usual crowd of well-wishers and second guessers out in the hallway. Nate and Hatch each gave a knowing smile and started to walk to the elevator.

"Mr. Keller, Mr. Keller," came the Spanish accented voice of the district clerk. Nate paused and turned around as the clerk breathlessly rushed up to him.

"Here's a certified copy of the judgment," she said. "No charge," as she smiled. Nate accepted it gracefully but couldn't help remembering how he, unlike every other lawyer in the courthouse, had been denied the use of her copy machine during the trial. He'd been compelled to use the coin operated machine in the basement, three floors down, to make copies. Also, he had to keep about five dollars in quarters in his pockets.

As the district clerk left, Nate was summoned by Judge Jackson's secretary. As he entered the judge's office, Jackson was out of his robe sitting on the edge of his desk.

"Thanks for stopping by Mr. Keller. I just wanted to tell you I thought you did a great job. I thought we worked together pretty well. You know I've always been a big supporter of the Bar. Maybe you'll mention that to the folks up in Austin."

With that Jackson held out his hand which Nate shook.

Judge Jackson then said, "Well we really took care of ol' Edgar, didn't we?"

Nate couldn't think of any kind of a fitting response so he smiled and said, "Thank you judge," and left the room, thinking to himself, *you couldn't write a book about this place – no one would ever believe it. I've got to get out of here to preserve my sanity.*

McKenzie, of course, appealed but they were all fruitless. The Court of Appeals affirmed the trial court without oral argument, the state supreme court refused the application for a writ and the U.S. Supreme Court denied Edgar's application for *certiorari.*

Nate was back in Austin handling his case load and dealing with the appeals. Jen had entered her final semester and had classes only Monday through Thursday. She stayed in Austin Thursday night until Monday morning. She and Nate had planned a June wedding and, in the interim, had set up housekeeping in his rental house. Cat had persisted in his neighborhood patrols. Neither Jen nor Nate had it in their heart to leave Cat and since it was apparent that Cat was not inclined to give up his routine, at least for the time being, they would make Nate's rental their home. The vet clinic, where Jen had interned, was happy to offer her a permanent position upon graduation. Jen proceeded to make Nate's bachelor pad a home. Curtains, new paint, new furniture, regular meals, etc. Both Nate and Cat adjusted.

While Jen was in town, Cat concluded his evening tours early enough to come in and lay in Jen's lap when she and Nate stayed in. In any event, Cat always slept at Jen's feet. He had added the role of her protector to his already busy schedule. As to Nate, he was, as always, condescending.

During spring break, Nate and Jen stayed with her parents in Dallas. Jen's father was a UT graduate and a Longhorn fan, so he and Nate were soon engaged in orange blood sports. It was obvious to Nate that anything his daughter wanted his daughter got. So, if she wanted to live her life with this man, it was fine with him. Jen's mother proved a bit more difficult. Nate helped her clear the table, complimented her on her home, her cooking, and just about everything else Nate could think of. It was a full-frontal assault which by the third day saw her full capitulation when she invited him into the kitchen for his opinion of her sauce for beef wellington. Should she use port or just a red dinner wine?

That evening as they were retiring to their separate bedrooms, Jen punched Nate in his ribs.

He gasped, "What was that for?"

"You should be ashamed of yourself Mr. Nathaniel Longfellow Keller for the way you have shamelessly charmed my mom," replied Jen with a grin on her face. "What did you say to her when she asked about the wine?"

Nate drew himself up to his full height and with an attempted studious mien, which was betrayed by the beginning of a smile at his lips, replied. "Well, I think I said something like, I know there is a difference of opinion, but I personally prefer port."

"Had you ever even had Beef Wellington?" asked Jen.

"I didn't even know what it was."

He received another poke in the ribs as Jen said, "Nate, you're so full of it. I didn't know you could be so devious."

"I'll do whatever it takes to get my woman," responded Nate smiling.

Whereupon Jen threw her arms around his neck and whispered, "You've got your woman." This was followed by a long hard kiss until Jen finally pulled away saying, "we have to remember why we are in separate bedrooms."

Days later, Nate was working at his desk when his secretary buzzed him and said there was an FBI agent by the name of Hatch on the line. Surprised and somewhat puzzled, Nate picked up his phone.

"Hi, Tom, what's up?"

"How you doing?" said Hatch. Without waiting for a response, he continued, "Do you remember that McKenzie case down in the Valley?"

"Yeah, of course, the last appeal was final just a few weeks ago. Why are you asking?"

"You remember Noe Flores, the kid that McKenzie wanted a hit on? He was found shot to death day before yesterday."

Hatch's habit of asking questions and then not waiting for an answer could become annoying, thought Nate. Another thought was, *so why is he telling me this?* "Why are you telling me this, I mean, it's interesting but I'm sure you have a lot more important things on your plate."

"Well, here's the thing. The Sheriff has arrested McKenzie, and McKenzie says he won't talk to anyone but you."

"Man, that's crazy, that's a criminal case. The State Bar has no jurisdiction – I'm not in private practice – I can't represent him, even if I wanted to. There's nothing I can do for him."

"I know, but you might be able to do something for us. Look, my boss put me on this case because of possible cartel involvement. That's looking less and less likely, but I still have a little time and I'd like to get to the bottom of this. Edgar swears he wasn't involved. I know they all say that, but I was thinking if he'll talk to you, maybe we could close this thing out."

"Tom, I don't know, I'm paid to prosecute lawyers, not help the FBI solve cases. Don't get me wrong, I wouldn't mind helping, you helped me, but I just don't see how I can."

"How about taking a few days off and coming down and enjoying the springtime delights of the Valley? The government will cover your expenses. I know I'm asking a lot, but this case is like a burr under my saddle."

"Well, when a good Mormon boy from Utah starts talking Texan, I guess I understand you're serious. OK I don't have any trials for a couple of weeks, I'll ask my boss for a few days personal leave. Where do we meet?"

"McKenzie's in the county jail waiting on a bond hearing. Let's meet day after tomorrow at Tony's office at ten o'clock."

"See ya then."

Nate spotted Hatch's government car as he drove up, so he parked next to it. Nate and Hatch exchanged pleasantries as they entered the office of the sheriff.

"Any problems?" asked Hatch. "You know; with your boss or your lady?"

"Well," replied Nate, "I can't say either was thrilled, but neither said 'no,' so I'm good."

Catalon met them at the door to his office. He did not seem thrilled to see either of them. Taking the initiative, Hatch explained that Nate was here working with him, and they wanted to talk to McKenzie but first they would like a little background. He made it clear to Catalon; they were not second-guessing his case. The FBI's interest was in drugs. Somewhat mollified, Catalon invited them into his office. After declining coffee, they settled into chairs in front of Tony's desk.

"OK," he said, "what do you all want to know."

Hatch said, "I guess everything, why don't you just start at the beginning when your office got involved."

"Well about a week ago, the dispatcher took a call from the rural mail carrier whose route is out southwest of town on County Road 53. Before the war, a bunch of wetbacks formed a little colony out there, still five or six houses left around there. The mailman told the dispatcher that things seemed strange out at Noe's place. He never got any mail, but he always cleaned the circulars and stuff out of his mailbox, but his mailbox was full, and it looked like his old pickup hadn't moved in a week. Said he thought it looked suspicious. The dispatcher told one of the deputies to drive over that way and check it out. So, after a while he calls back on his radio and says there's a dead body in Noe's old home place. The body's in bad shape. The doors are all open and it looked like feral hogs had been at the body. Between that and the decomposition, all he could say for sure was that it was a male. Couldn't tell if it was Noe. Them damn hogs are big and they're all over the county – can't get rid of 'em even though there's a bounty on 'em."

"Anyway, so I call the medical examiner and my investigator, and I drive out there. The county road is gravel and oyster shell, but Noe's driveway is just mud after some recent showers. The house sits back about thirty yards from the road. As I get out of my car, I see a set of footprints between the road and the house. I call the deputy who made the discovery, and he says the prints aren't his – they were there when he arrived. I have my investigator measure and photograph them."

"We go into the house, and we find a body on its back lying just inside the front doorway. There's a large hole in the forehead and there's another hole in the chest. We both are pretty sure its Noe. We search the place and don't find a thing, no prints, no shell casings, nothing. All we got is the body and footprints. We photograph everything and then I turn the body over to the medical examiner."

"He does an autopsy and finds what he says are two .38 caliber slugs in the body which he identifies from fingerprints as belonging to Noe Flores. But because of the decomposition and the ravage caused by the animals, he can't give a time of death."

"So, my logical suspect is McKenzie. He tried to have Noe killed once before so maybe now he's decided to do it himself. Me and a couple of deputies drive over to Edgar's house. He opens the door in his stocking feet. About that time, the deputy I sent to watch the rear door comes around to the front with Edgar's boots in his hand. They're caked with mud."

"I read McKenzie his rights and he agrees to talk to me. Says he hasn't been out of the house in days and has no idea how the mud got on his boots. He seems genuinely surprised to hear of Noe's murder, claims to know nothing of it. I tell him not to leave town and since his boots were in plain sight on the back porch, I am seizing them as possible evidence."

"We get a soil sample from Noe's place and take a sample from Edgar's boots and send them off for analysis. The report comes back. They are the same. So, I get a search warrant and I find a .38 caliber Smith & Wesson police special in a cardboard box on Edgar's desk in his study. We seize it and send the slugs off to the DPS along with the handgun which we can tell has been recently fired and has two empty shell casings in its chamber. The report comes back, the slugs from the body match the ones test fired from McKenzie's revolver. We arrest Edgar and charge him with intentional homicide. Seems to me we got an open and shut case."

"Sounds pretty good," said Hatch. "Can we talk to Edgar?"

"I've contacted Mia, as Noe's next of kin. She's pretty shook -up, as you'd expect. Thinks the cartel was behind it. I didn't tell her otherwise – didn't want to upset her anymore. You want to talk to him? Okay, I'll have him brought up."

The man ushered into the interrogation room bears but scant resemblance to the proud and confident person of the trial. Time in jail and baloney sandwiches twice a day would do that to you, thought Nate.

McKenzie looked at each man in turn and said, "thanks for coming. I know both of you think I'm a piece of shit and I understand that. To be honest with you, I kinda agree with you. I was just flat-ass crazy – I mean that woman – I don't know – I couldn't stand sharing her but when it dawned on me that I'd been played, I have to tell you I was relieved. There's no way after all that I would kill Flores. Hell, I ain't that dumb. I don't even know where he lived."

Nate and Tom sat silently as McKenzie unburdened himself. Finally, Hatch said, "you said you could give up some information on the cartel. Let's talk about that."

"I can and will but first you gotta get this murder charge off my back."

Nate said, "I'm not sure why I'm here Edgar. You have a lawyer working on your bail. I can't represent you – I'm not sure I should even be talking to you."

"Mr. Keller, Nate, if I may, thank you for coming, my lawyer is only working on bail. I don't have a lawyer representing me on the charges. I know you can't represent me, probably wouldn't anyway, but I have to say you really impressed me, you didn't back off once you had the bit in your mouth and let me say I have no idea who made those threats, they were stupid. I had nothing to do with them. Anyway, as I was saying, you seemed to be a fair person and beyond question a person who believes in justice. I'm being set up. The people around here were impressed by you. They'll talk to you. Please, please help me."

"Well, I'll listen to your side," said Nate, "I'm already here anyway."

"Shit! that's just it," said Edgar." I don't have a side. I don't know what the hell's going on."

"Your pistol fired the fatal shots. The Sheriff says your boots made the tracks. You'd tried to have Noe killed, pretty bad set of facts."

"Don't I know it. Let's start with the gun. No prints, if I was dumb enough to leave it on my desk with two spent shells, why would I bother to wipe it for prints? My prints should have been on that gun. Someone got it, used it, then wiped it off, and put it back. Now I can't tell you how someone could have done all that, but I swear someone did."

"Where was it?" said Nate.

"They found it in a cardboard box on my desk in my study."

"What was it doing there?"

"Well, after the trial, I was barred from my office. Someone boxed all my personal things up, including the gun, I guess. I didn't even look in the box, I just set it on my desk and as far as I know, it sat there until the sheriff found it. I don't think I even went into my study after setting the box down – had no reason to."

"OK, couple of questions. Who delivered the box and when?" asked Nate.

"Let's see, yeah, Tony himself brought it over with a big smug grin. I don't recall when, but it was fairly recently. I hadn't missed anything in there, so I didn't pay much attention. I think Tony said he had to wait until the appeals were over. I remember thinking that made no sense but if you know Tony, he's got his own ideas about things. Didn't really think any more about it to tell the truth."

"How about the footprints and matching mud on your boots?" said Hatch.

"Well, I don't have no ideas how that mud got on my boots. I always leave them at the back door. My wife says they scratch her wood floors, so I don't wear them in the house."

Nate and Hatch took their leave and went back to Catalon's office and got permission to view the boots and photographs of the scene. After thanking Catalon for his cooperation, they stopped on the street outside the jail.

"What do you think?" asked Hatch. "Don't know yet, let's drive by Edgar's house," said Nate.

They drove into an older but well-maintained neighborhood of the city. They finally located the McKenzie house. It was built of white concrete brick, ranch style, not new but not too old either. There were flower beds and a manicured lawn. The house itself was located on a corner lot. As they drove around the corner, they could see a white Ford LTD, sitting in the driveway in front of a detached two-car garage. It was connected to the house by a covered breezeway. The sidewalk from the garage led to three concrete steps which in turn led up to a concrete porch about a dozen feet square. To the right of the door and near the edge of the porch was affixed a black cast-iron boot scraper.

Nate and Hatch looked at each other. "Why wouldn't Edgar scrape the mud off his boots rather than just let them dry with mud on them?" asked Hatch. "Just what I was wondering," said Nate. "I also noticed the porch is clearly visible and close to the street. The house across the street is screened by tall hedges. Someone could have taken his boots and returned them sight unseen. Not likely, maybe, but not impossible either."

"So, what's next?"

"Unless you've got something to add, I'd say tomorrow we need to talk to Mia, we need to see who at the Sheriff's office received Edgar's things from his office, and we need to see Noe's house," said Nate.

"Sounds about right," said Hatch. "You ready for a beer?"

Chapter 11 – Fire and Murder

A thunderous explosion rattled the windows of his room just after midnight and abruptly awakened Nate. Before he could even crawl out of bed, his room phone rang.

It was Hatch. “Get dressed, we gonna go.”

“What’s up?”

“Tell you on the way!”

Nate threw on his clothes and joined Hatch in his car.

As he jammed his foot on the Ford’s gas petal, Hatch explained, “There was some kind of an explosion and fire at the ranch supply store out in the county at the edge of the city. The explosion has spread the flames and apparently the fire is threatening to spread to the rest of the strip center. Seems like the local volunteer fire department is overwhelmed and with its resources can only fight a delaying action while it waits for assistance from neighboring departments. The Sheriff called me,” Hatch continued as the car spun around a corner, “he’s pretty upset. Said all his deputies as well as the city police are tied up working traffic, crowd control and checking out nearby buildings to warn and rescue occupants. He thinks the explosion and fire were suspicious and he asked me to look around and see what I could find. Rousting you was my idea, I figured if I couldn't sleep you couldn’t either,” Hatch added with a grin on his face.

"Thanks," Nate answered, without any enthusiasm whatsoever.

As they arrived at the scene, it became obvious the flames were out of control. They soared upwards for fifty or sixty feet casting a huge red and orange canopy in the starless night. The sound of the inferno was like a freight train running full throttle, thought Nate. The heat was so intense that the paint on a car across the street was beginning to blister. The volunteers on the two local pumpers were valiantly spraying streams of water around the edges but otherwise couldn't do much but watch the conflagration. There was no hope at this time of doing any kind of investigation as to its origin.

Even at this unholy hour, a crowd had begun to form, many of whom were owners of nearby businesses. They besieged anyone in authority for information. There was none to be had.

The local police and sheriff's deputies were using flashlights in their efforts to keep the crowd back and to check on adjoining buildings. Other than these and the fire itself, there was no light as Hatch and Nate sought out the Sheriff. They eventually found him conferring with the mayor and the chief of the fire department. All were soot covered and their voices were husky. The chief was saying the business stored fertilizer which would ignite with fuel and an oxidizer but would otherwise be inert. Arson was a possibility because in his opinion ammonium nitrate in granular form was most unlikely to spontaneously explode.

Presently, Tony spotted Hatch standing nearby and asked his opinion.

"There needs to be a full-scale investigation to be sure, but on the appearance of it, I'd tend to agree with the chief,"

Hatch replied. “Something as common as kerosene together with a large blasting cap or a little stick of dynamite can be set off remotely by a device as simple as a radio control for a model airplane. The truth is it doesn’t take a rocket scientist with elaborate equipment. What we are really left with is who and why?”

The answer to one question was answered shortly when the Sheriff received a call from the jail. He stepped away from the others as he listened to his dispatcher on the handheld radio. His face turned from shock to disbelief as he listened.

“Ten four,” he said as he rejoined the others. “McKenzie’s been shot dead in his jail cell. The door to the back parking lot is open and Lonnie, the jailor on duty, is missing. He and the dispatcher were the only two at the jail. I had to pull all on duty deputies, even those off duty, to the scene of the fire. McKenzie was the only prisoner since the contractor for the Department of Corrections earlier today ... well, I guess now, it was yesterday, took away all those inmates who had been convicted and sentenced to prison. I smell a rat. This damn fire and the killing can’t be a coincidence. I gotta get back to the jail.”

With that he sprinted (more like a trot) to his car.

Hatch and Nate got Lonnie’s home address from the dispatcher and took off in Hatch’s Ford, while the sheriff returned to his office ... now a crime scene.

Lonnie lived alone in an old apartment complex of two stories with two longitudinal arms and one across the rear. An open area between the two wings apparently was intended at one time to be a grassy lawn surrounding a swimming pool. It was now just stubble. The pool was empty of water and served as a convenient trash collector; old newspapers, beer bottles, fast food wrappers, leaves and tree branches had collected on its bottom. The units were built of wood and in need of paint. The complex was long out of style and its overall appearance was one of fatigue.

Hatch and Nate climbed the rickety stairs to the second level of the western arm of the complex and soon located Lonnie's unit. The door was ajar with a pool of dark coppery-smelling liquid staining the sticky carpet, softly glistening in the dim light from the interior.

"It's blood," Hatch murmured. Nate nodded in agreement. He was in no doubt at all. The smell of blood – all too familiar to him. Doubtless also to Tom Hatch. Hatch drew his weapon, a Smith and Westen 442 air weight .38 caliber revolver. With Nate close behind, Hatch skirted the pool of dark liquid and stepped into the apartment. Carefully, with weapon drawn, he swiftly checked the bedroom and bath of the small unit.

"All clear," he murmured as he returned to the body by the doorway, Hatch bent down and checked a carotid artery.

"Is he dead?" Nate kept his voice to a whisper.

"As a doornail," Tom replied, also in a whisper, "But not for very long."

Next to Lonnie's body lay a Colt model 1911 .45 semi-automatic pistol. With his handkerchief, Tom picked up the weapon, sniffed the barrel, removed the magazine and popped out the unspent cartridges. Nate, standing next to him spotted a spent shell casing on the floor. Using his pocketknife, he bent down, picked it up and handed it to Hatch. Hatch wrapped it, the pistol and magazine in his handkerchief and stowed them in one of his coat pockets.

"Looks like Lonnie got off one round and judging by the pool of blood at the doorway, it did some damage," Hatch observed. "I'm calling it in to the police and sheriff. There's a trail of blood toward the back stairway. Here, take this," Hatch added. as he bent down and retrieved a Smith and Wesson 642 air weight hammerless .38 revolver from an ankle holster.

"I thought only the bad guys carried hidden guns," said Nate.

"So do the smart good guys," Hatch replied. "You've only got five rounds, I've got some reloads so stick with me," he ordered, and started toward the rear stairs.

"Shouldn't we wait for backup?" asked Nate.

Moving forward, Hatch said over his shoulder, "Have you seen a local cop or deputy you'd trust for backup?"

"Not lately," Nate admitted, honestly. "Let's go."

"Looks like whoever put Lonnie down is bleeding pretty badly. Wherever that .45 slug hit him it would have left a big hole, so he's hurting," Hatch surmised. "Probably going to go to ground around here somewhere so keep your eyes open."

The two cautiously crept down the stairway and moved into the darkness in between the front and rear buildings relieved to be out of the dim glow cast by the light above the stairs. Once into the darkness they crouched side by side, each trying to pierce the darkness that now enveloped them.

"Where do you think he went?" whispered Nate.

"I think to the left," responded Hatch. "There's nothing but mesquite trees and underbrush to the rear – not easy going plus it don't lead anywhere. This guy's hurting and wants to get some help. My guess is he's got a car out there he's trying to get to."

"It would probably be to the left then," Nate ventured, "That would be the nearest roadway and the best place to park next to Lonnie's apartment."

"I agree," said Hatch. "My eyes are getting used to the dark. Looks like a stack pile of logs next door. Plenty of places to hide. You go left and I'll go right, you drive him to me. Be careful, just wait for him."

With that they moved out and entered what indeed was a fence post supply lot. Cedar logs in seven-foot lengths, which would allow their proper height above ground of four and a half feet for cattle fencing, were stacked in neat squares with narrow pathways between them. The stacks were seven or eight feet high and seemed, from ground level, to extend forever. As Nate and Hatch separated and crept into the maze there was a sudden loud crack of gunfire and the thud of a bullet lodging into a log.

Hatch shouted out, "give it up! We're cops and we have you surrounded! There's nowhere for you to go!"

The response was another loud report and a bee-like buzzing overhead. Then close on its heels came the sound of shuffling. The object of their search was nearby but still dangerous. Hatch moved to his right and then his left and Nate crept ahead slowly wishing he could see something. All at once he rounded the corner of a stack of logs and the distant light of the huge fire revealed a dark mass in the pathway ahead. Just as he had spotted the dark shape it began to revolve toward him, and he briefly caught a flash of reflected light. Nate instinctively thrust his revolver up and forward and squeezed the trigger. The report of his weapon rang in his ears, but he still caught the sound of a cry from the dark mass ahead. As Nate carefully took a step or two forward, he could see the shape in front now appeared to be upon the ground. Reaching it, there was just enough light to discern the shape of a body.

Just then Hatch called out, “Nate, you OK?”

“Yeah, think so, the guy’s down.”

Hatch appeared and using the small light on his keyring, he illuminated the shape. It was the body of a young Mexican, lying on his back, a Colt super .38 auto in his right outstretched arm. Hatch quickly kicked away the weapon and bent down to check for vitals. Nate stared momentarily dazed.

Hatch stood up, pretending not to notice Nate’s distress, and said, “Great shot, you got him in the neck. He was dead before he hit the ground.”

“He’s just a kid,” said Nate, “I didn’t even aim just pointed and shot.”

“That’s the best way at a time and place like this. He’s a typical *pistolaro*. The cartel gets these poor kids, throws money at them, applauds and rewards them until they think they are bullet proof. They are, in effect, brainwashed so that they have no regard for human life. They just become killing machines. So, don’t be concerned about taking a young life. It was hardly a human one anyway. I hear sirens close by. Lay down your gun and put your hands up and let’s walk out to the street, we don’t want these good guys with guns to shoot us by mistake.”

Later at Catalon’s office, after the debriefing by Hatch and Nate, the Sheriff said,

“My turn now. I’ve called Austin for the state arson investigator. He’ll be here tomorrow. I have no doubt but that the fire was set to draw law enforcement away from the jail. I have to admit I never suspected Lonnie, but he obviously was the only one who could have let the hit man in the jail. I’d heard rumors that Edgar was on the take by the cartel. Couldn’t prove it, of course. My guess is Lonnie heard Edgar say he would open up about the cartel if you two could get the murder rap off his back. Lonnie then must have passed it on and maybe when he thought about loose ends being taken care of, he realized he was a loose end. So, he takes off. We searched his apartment and found $30,000.00 in the cushions of his couch. He musta swung by his apartment to grab the money and was caught there by the *pistolaro*. There is no record anywhere on him so we have no clue as to who he was or where he came from. Musta been a pretty tough kid, took a .45 slug through the door into his left side just above the hip. Hada hurt like a bitch, he still kicks the cheap door in and does Lonnie. Then tries to get away. We found a car we think he used out on the street a little past the cedar post place. It was stolen, of course. So, the trail is pretty much cold."

"Thanks for filling us in," said Hatch. "Any problem about the shooting?"

"Nah," said the Sheriff, "I already had a sit down with the D.A., Hell, he ain't even gonna take it to the grand jury."

Hatch looked over at Nate, "You look like you want to say something."

"Not really, I guess I'm sitting here thinking what a near thing it was. If the kid hadn't had a shiny stainless-steel pistol so that the light flashed off it when he raised it in my direction, I'd probably be dead. I could never have made that shot – as it was if my bullet had gone one inch to the left I'd missed him and he probably would have tagged me."

"Well, we humans don't know why the Lord arranges things as he does. When they work in our favor, all we can do is give thanks. I'm bushed, let's get back to the motel and grab a couple of hours sleep," said Tom.

Chapter 12 – The Ghosts of 'Nam

Later that afternoon Tom and Nate met at the motel coffee shop. They each ordered coffee and hamburgers.

Tom looked at Nate, "You OK? If you don't mind my saying so, you look like hell."

"Feel like it too. That business this morning brought back some things I thought I'd gotten past."

"You mean, 'Nam?" "Yeah", said Nate.

"I know what you mean," said Hatch.

"You too?"

"S2 intelligent officer one five first Marine. Hue. I was POG but you know every gyrene is trained as a rifleman. We were losing people so fast the skipper put everybody on the street."

"Man, you guys ran into a shitstorm."

"Tell me about it. There's this one thing that keeps flashing into my head when I don't expect it. It's like on a tape that just keeps looping around. It's weird. I don't have nightmares, or anything, it's like a song or a name that pops up in your head and you can't get it out of your mind all day long. I've learned to live with it though. Anyway, I'm going room to room clearing this house with my fire team when I turn a corner and there's this skinny guy wearing a U.C. Berkley T shirt. He's wearing shorts and basketball sneakers with the Nike *swoosh* logo on them. Looks like he's about to go shoot some baskets except he has an AK-47 in his hands. He's looking out a window but, I guess he hears me coming, I see him just as he's starting to turn. I'm on full auto and I empty the rest of my clip and I just tear him into a bloody mess."

"Strange shit goes on in a war," says Nate. "Unlike you I do have this one nightmare. I'm leading my platoon down the trail when suddenly, I fall into this hole that is covered with grass. Just at that time, a RPG round takes off my radioman's head. He's just behind me so I got showered with parts of his brain, blood, bone and all that stuff. It's so real I can smell that stuff."

"Man, I can see how that might have comeback. You seeing anybody for those things?" questioned Hatch.

"Nah. Like I said, after I met Jen, they went away. I'm hoping this was a one-of-a-kind thing, you know. Triggered by the shootout. I'm really okay about that, it simply was him or me. So, let's get on with it."

"Nate, the mind's a strange thing. We see agents with problems, I mean veteran agents, so it's no big deal to have a talk about it."

"No, no, I'm good."

"Well, okay if you say so," said Hatch, "looks to me like the reason we came down here, just ended. McKenzie sure as shootin' ain't gonna tell us about anything."

"I know, but since I'm down here and after looking at the sheriff's case against McKenzie I'm not sure he's the right person. I'd like to keep digging."

"Glad to hear it," said Hatch, "Me too. Where do you want to start?"

"Not much time left today," Nate replied. "I'd say we run by the courthouse before it closes and find out when and who removed McKenzie's things from his office. Then maybe go over to Catalon's office and get directions to Noe's place, directions to Mia's place across the river and then I'd like to take another look at Edgar's boots and the pictures. Something's bugging me about those boots but I can't figure out what exactly."

"Sounds about right to me. I'm thinking we both pretty much agree about Edgar. He might not have been as smart as he thought he was, but he isn't so stupid as to kill somebody and leave the murder weapon on his desk. Tony, to me, seemed happy to pin it on Edgar. So happy, he never even conducted an investigation in any sense of the word."

"We're on the same page partner, drink up and let's go," said Nate.

They made their way to the office of the district attorney, where they managed to track down the receipt for Edgar's personal possessions. The document disclosed that the box had been delivered to the sheriff's office a good two weeks prior to any possible date of Noe's death. Back in Tom's government car, the two discussed the significance of this discovery.

"Why would Tony hold onto the box so long," Nate wondered out loud. "Guess we'd better ask. Also, where was it in his office and who might have had access to it. After all, since we don't know the exact date of Noe's murder, that box with Edgar's gun in it ... that opens up a new can of worms."

Tony was out when they arrived at his office. They waited a good 45 minutes until unannounced, Tony entered his office. He offered no apology nor explanation and his raised eyebrows suggested he expected an explanation for their presence.

"Sheriff, I don't want to be a nuisance, but my boss wants a full report covering everything, so I just have a few loose ends to run down," said Hatch. "If you could bear with me a little longer, I'll be out of your hair real soon."

"Okay, I understand that. But what do you need from me?" Catalon said while looking pointedly at Nate.

"I've talked Nate into helping me. Two heads and two memories are better than one, you know." Tom Hatch quickly recognized the reason for the Sheriff's stare. "If you have an address for Mia Flores, we would like to have it."

The Sheriff took a seat behind his desk without indicating whether he was satisfied with the explanation or not. At any rate, he quickly responded to Hatch's request. Taking a legal pad from a desk drawer, Catalon began drawing a map.

"Okay, here's the bridge that leads to Reynosa, then you go here," He pointed to what he had drawn. "Turn right and keep going here. This is her address," he added, writing the street name and building number down on his map. "Here's her telephone number, in case you needed it."

Sheriff Catalon apparently noticed the glance that passed between Nate and Hatch, and quickly explained, "I obtained this information when Keller requested her appearance as a witness at the McKenzie's trial. I don't know any other address in Reynosa, so I guess this just stuck in my mind."

"I appreciate that," Tom Hatch replied, although he sounded skeptical. "That will help us a lot. I am wondering now why so much time passed between the time McKenzie's possessions were obtained by your office and the time they were returned to him. Who all had access to them during this period?"

"Why do you want to know? I can't see how its relevant to anything!" Sheriff Catalon demanded.

"You're probably right," Tom Hatch attempted to mollify the sheriff. "But my boss is one of those guys who likes to micromanage. I'd be really grateful if you'd help me out here."

"One of my deputies, I don't remember which one or when, but one of them received the box from McKenzie's office and gave it to me. I was busy and put the box on top of the file cabinet over there(pointing) and I just forgot about it. Then one day – I can't remember when – but the date will be on the receipt signed by McKenzie, I just noticed the box and decided to get it out of my office. So I grabbed the box and drove over to McKenzie's place and handed it to him. I didn't even look in the box – I have no idea what was in it – I'd guess the contents were listed on an inventory sheet in the box. Anyway, as I recall McKenzie didn't look in the box either, just signed our office receipt form." With a grunt and a grimace, Tony Catalon dug into a bottom desk drawer and laid the paper receipt on his desk with a look of pained resignation. "Here's the receipt, but since the date of Noe's death is unknown, I don't see how this makes any difference. Now is that all?"

That wasn't all, even though both Tom and Nate could see they were nearing the end of the Sheriff's patience.

Nate asked, "Do you have a map out to Noe's place?"

Catalon raised his eyebrows and uttered a profanity under his breath but didn't bother asking why they needed a map to Noe's place. With every nonverbal indication at this command, Catalon was a man about to explode, but instead, thinking *compliance might be the quickest way to rid himself of these tormentors,* Catalon drew a sketch and pushed it across his desk.

While doing so, he added the most dreaded words everyone who has ever asked for directions ever heard, "You can't miss it." Catalon did add clarification. "After his parents passed on, Noe didn't spend much time or money keeping up the place. When the roof began to leak, he used an old 'Clabber Girl' metal sign he found somewhere to patch it. The neighbors started calling it the 'Clabber Girl House' cause this sign on the roof is clearly visible a good ways down the road."

Nate, knowing he was tempting fate, ventured one more question. "Did you ask any of the neighbors if they had seen anything strange or heard any noise around the time, we think Noe was killed?" As Nate had feared, this was one question too many. Tony rose with fists doubled up and placed them in the middle of his desk.

In a voice several decibels louder than necessary to emphasize his displeasure, Sheriff Catalon stated, "No Goddamn, I did not Goddamn ask anybody a Goddamn thing – I had my Goddamn murderer. Now, if that's all, I got Goddamn things to do."

Hatch and Nate mumbled a quick thanks and rapidly retreated to Hatch's Ford.

"I think we pissed him off," Hatch commented.

"Really? What gave you the clue?" said Nate laughing.

With a grin on his face, Tom Hatch asked, "What did you think of his instant memory about Mia?"

"I thought it pretty odd, but I guess his explanation is plausible. But what's strange to me is why did he think he needed an explanation? Sounds kinda defensive to me."

"Yeah, you're right," Tom Hatch agreed, "Seemed that way to me too. We didn't ask to see the boots and footprints; want to go back?"

"Tony might throw us in jail if we do. The boots bothered me, but I don't guess I need to see them again. I remember now what it was that concerned me; We talked about how dumb it was not to clean the boots but more importantly to me was two other things I noticed about them. First, on the right foot there was a crease above the ankle. That crease had dried mud on it as though it had rested on the ground. Now there was mud out there, but no one said it was ever like a swamp. To me, I just can't see how if Edgar really was wearing these boots, he would have caused a crease above his ankle. And how could that part of his boot above his ankle, have come down into the mud. Another thing I noticed in the photos of the footprints – indentions at the top of several of them. They were wider at the top than the others and looked like something had pressed down on their right side."

"So, what are you getting at?" Tom Hatch seemed genuinely interested in Nate's observations.

"Just this, and I could be wrong," said Nate, "But what if a person whose foot is too small for the boots tried to walk in them? The mud could have held the boot back, retarded it a little, causing that person to sort of step out of the boot. Then to not step out of the boot completely or to keep from falling, wouldn't that person step down on the side of the boot? I've been thinking and that's the only logical explanation I can come up with is that accounts for the crease in the boot, the mud in the crease, and the indentation in the footprints. Can you think of another?"

"I see what you're saying," said Tom Hatch. He paused a while and then continued, "I can't think of any other explanation either. I think we also need to throw into the mix that obvious thing about Sheriff Catalon – his disproportionate small feet. Coupled with the fact he had possession of the murder weapon during a time it could have been used. Then add in the fact that he made absolutely no attempt to investigate the killing but simply latched onto the obvious. Having said that, however, why would he do it – what's his motive?"

"I don't know. Maybe Mia or a visit to the scene will help. If not, then I can't see where else we can go. Suspicion alone of Tony Catalon won't clear this case," said Nate.

"You're right. Let's get a fresh start in the morning. I'd say we check out Mia first. Ready for a beer?"

"Always."

Chapter 13 – Mia's Revelations

The next morning Hatch and Nate drove south over the international bridge into Mexico. Following Tony's sketch, they soon left the well paved main highway and turned into a warren of city streets, some with narrow pavement, some with none, all marred by potholes with litter along the roadside. Soon their car was besieged by urchins of all sizes and sexes tapping on the car windows and darting in front of it demanding "*dinero*," "*dinero*."

"Don't give them any," Tom Hatch advised, "You'll just attract more and pretty soon we won't even be able to move without driving over one or two."

"Yeah, I know. Have you thought any more about Tony?"

The drumming noise inside the car was now making it difficult to hear one another but Tom Hatch raised his voice and said, "I thought about him off and on all night long. Haven't come to a decision. I like him so maybe I'm giving him too much slack. I don't know."

"I know what you mean. I feel the same way, but I keep coming back to him. We don't have another suspect."

"Well," said Hatch, "I don't know if we can totally rule out the cartel. There were always rumors about Noe being a part-time mule. Maybe he talked out of school or screwed up somehow. The cartel ain't interested in apologies."

"That's true," Nate admitted. "Guess we just have to keep digging."

"I think that might be Mia's place over there," said Hatch pointing. "She knows you better than me, so why don't you take her."

"That's okay with me," said Nate. "Are you sure we're in the right place. I haven't seen a street sign since we left the main highway."

"Only one way to find out," said Hatch as he stopped the car and began to step out.

As they left the car, the crowd of beggars began to recede. The cries for money died away as an extremely large and overweight Mexican approached. He was wheezing and attempting to catch his breath. With one hand he was dabbing at the sweat conspicuous on his forehead with a red and white bandana. In his other hand he was holding a black rumpled up cap with some sort of emblem on its front. He was wearing a light blue short-sleeve shirt which stuck to his body with large sweat stains beneath each arm. His trousers were a dark color and were not exactly clean. He had a badge on his left breast pocket. He did not appear to be armed and had no other sign of authority. The crowd melted away before him.

As he approached within several yards, he managed a smile and offered, "Watch your car, *por favor*?"

"*Si, gracias, regreso treinta minutos,*" replied Tom Hatch, as he reached in his pocket and handed him a handful of Mexican pesos.

"*Gracias,* I watch your car good," the fat man answered as he slowly turned side to side and glared at the ragged youngsters.

As they headed toward the building they were seeking, Nate asked, "Do you think he's a real cop? How much money did you give him?"

"Who knows, he seems to be the guy in charge around here, so I guess it makes no difference. I gave him fifty pesos – about two buck fifty American – should be enough to keep the tires on the car."

The two men entered the lobby of a three-story concrete building. The sign on the exterior was covered in graffiti as was most of the front on either side of the double glass doors. Immediately to their front as they entered was an elevator with a "*fuera de servicio*" sign across it. To the right was a stairway. As they moved toward it a Mexican in an outfit similar to the one worn by their car watcher hurriedly emerged from a door to their left.

"*El alto; cual estu negocio?"*

He was much smaller than his partner outside, but he was wearing some kind of a revolver in a scarred-up leather holster on his belt. There was no badge on his left breast. Apparently whatever authority he possessed emanated from the object on his hip.

Hatch flipped open his credentials and said, "*FBI comprehende? Habla English*?"

"Si, FBI I understand little."

"What's your name?" asked Nate.

"Alejandro."

"You a guard or something?"

"Si, I protect building. I live back there (pointing to the door he had entered from). *Mi esposa* and *dos ninos*."

"Do you know Mia Flores, is she in her apartment?" Tom Hatch handed Alejandro forty pesos.

"Gracias," said Alejandro, with a large smile, "I think maybe so, I have not seen her leave."

"Great, we know the way, how 'bout you just stay here?" Tom Hatch suggested. Receiving no argument, they ascended the stairway. The building was showing its age, but seemed to be in fair shape, except for the elevator. It was clean inside, no graffiti anywhere inside. Nate guessed Alejandro's wife probably cleaned the lobby and stairs. They reached the third floor and walked down the worn but clean carpet to Mia's door. It had a bright brass number affixed to its lime exterior. It was several minutes until there was a response to their knock. Mia appeared at the door. She was barefoot wearing white shorts and a light blue chambray man's shirt, tied at her waist, obviously several sizes too large for her. *Noe's*, thought Nate. The shirt size did nothing to conceal her natural endowments. Although she was not tall, she had long supple legs for her size. Nate couldn't believe that he had never noticed how very pretty she was. *The trial must have really distracted me.* Even now with her black hair in tangles and her green eyes rimmed in by darkened circles, she still would turn heads.

"Yes, what is it?" she asked.

Gaining his wits, Nate said, "I'm Nate Keller; you were a witness for me at Edgar's trial, do you remember me?"

"*Si*, I know both of you, why are you here, what do you want?"

Tom Hatch responded, "We're looking into Noe's death, may we come in?"

Mia took her time, gazing at each of them in turn before, without a word, she moved back from the door and allowed them to enter. The room was not large and was furnished with inexpensive furniture, but everything was neat and clean. “Please have a seat,” Mia said.

“I remember from the trial, your English is very good,” said Nate.

“Noe help me and Edgar too and then Edgar got me into classes in a junior college across river. I go, I mean, I went two semesters.”

“We are very sorry to impose on you while you are mourning your husband but maybe you can help us find out who did it. So, do you mind if we ask you a few questions?”

“Is okay.”

“When was the last time you saw Noe alive?” asked Tom Hatch, “And was there anything strange about his behavior? I mean did he act like he was afraid or anything?”

“No, my Noe, he was always the same with me. Kind and gentle. We knew each other since we were kids. My mother did housework across the river and she would bring me with her. Noe’s father did yardwork for the same family and he would bring Noe. So, we just grew up together. I guess we were always in love and when we could do it legally, we got married but Noe could not settle down. He always had some big idea. He gonna be rich. I always wait for him, he make me happy. He would bring me money when he could, if he didn’t drink it up first or smoke it up. Noe had a side to him I could not understand but around me, he always acted happy and promised we could live together one day. I guess I talk too much, I miss him so.”

“That’s okay, we understand, -- do you remember when you saw him last?” Tom Hatch prodded gently.

“It must have been just before he got killed, I don’t remember the date. He came to see me and brought me a little money he had made from doing yardwork. He was so happy, he told me he was going to get a lot of money in a day or two and we could finally live together. You know he never said anything to me, but I know him, he never liked me seeing Edgar and taking his money. We were like simpatico – we didn't have to say things out loud – we just knew what the other one was thinking – he knew I did not like it either, but he was happy I didn't have to do housework any more like my mother had to do. We each did what we had to do hoping we could be together some day, you know what I mean?"

"Yes, I do," Tom Hatch answered, "Did he tell you where this money was coming from or why he was going to get it; was it a job or something?"

"No, job, all he told me, he said he was doing yardwork, and someone drove up and told him they were going to make things right for what Edgar tried to do to him."

"Man, woman, description?"

"Sorry, that's all he said, but he sounded as if it was going to happen soon. To tell the truth I didn't pay a lot of attention, it just sounded like another of Noe's dreams."

"So, that's it?"

"I'm afraid so. But there was a strange thing happen later. Tony came by and told me about Noe and said as his widow the funeral director needed instructions. This was, I think, the day after Tony said Noe was killed. I didn't know what to do, I had no money for a funeral. I mean I wanted my Noe to be cared for but what could I do? Tony, he drive me to the funeral home and the man in charge there says he has a letter for me. Inside is $2,000.00 and a note that tells me to use this for Noe's funeral."

"Was it signed, any kind of a name or address on it!" asked Hatch.

"No, no nothing. I give the money to the man there and he say it only pay for cremation. I don't like it but like always I don't have a choice."

"So, you have no idea who sent you the money?" asked Hatch. "How about the note?"

"I have no idea who sent it. I don't have the note."

"Do you think it might be the person that promised Noe money?"

"Maybe, I don't know."

"Do you know where he was working – whose yard he was working on the day he brought you the money? Did he have regular customers?"

"No, no, he never say, I don't know. I try to remember everything but I'm so worried – I have no money. I don't want to go back cleaning people's toilets, you know. Tony, he act like he want to help me but he not generous like Edgar. Tony, he give me $50.00 after we go to bed. But that's not enough – that won't pay the rent or buy groceries. So, I'm scared, I don't know what I'm gonna do."

"Sorry to break in," said Nate. "Do you mean Tony the sheriff?"

"*Si.*"

"How long, I mean you and he, since when?"

"Ever since he come by to be sure I will testify. He said Edgar was done – I couldn't depend on him no more – Tony, he said he would like to come over and see me now and then. I didn't much like him but I say okay, again I feel I have no choice. Turns out, like I say, he is not very kind. I think maybe I make a bad deal."

Hatch and Nate exchanged glances but before either could ask more questions, Mia said she remembered something else. She said before his last visit, maybe five or six days previously, Noe had come to see her very late at night. When she let him in, he told her to turn off the lights. He went to the window facing the street and looked out for a long time making a gesture for her to be quiet. After a while, they went to bed, and he told her he had to leave early in the morning to try and cross the river. He said some drug guys might be after him – he had heard talk of it.

"I ask him why they were after him. He look down and tell me he sometimes carry things across the river for them. A couple of days ago they give him some weed to carry over. He say he punched a small hole in the packet and squeezed some out and smoked it. It was so little he didn't think anyone would notice. But they did, and word got back to him that these guys were looking for him. He scare me but he tell me it gonna be okay. I was so happy when he came back to see me. He tell me was nothing to worry about – just talk. But now I have to wonder, you know?"

Further questions revealed nothing else of importance and Hatch and Nate took their leave. They were silent, each with his own thoughts as they made their way back to their car.

Finally, as they were crossing the bridge back to Texas, Hatch spoke up. "Well, all that sort of scrambles things up. We got a motive for Tony. Now we know he had a reason, the means, and opportunity to get rid of Noe and put the blame on Edgar. But we also now get some new players. It had to be the cartel Noe was involved with. They have the drug business locked down. They are the only players around here. What do you make of it all?"

"I agree with everything you said," answered Nate. "Certainly, Tony has to be a person of interest. I pretty much discount a cartel hit. But as I say that I suppose Lonnie could have gotten Edgar's gun and given it to the cartel hit man – maybe the kid I shot. Lonnie could have known about Edgar's habit of leaving his boots on the back porch. If the cartel did it – it's a dead-end – their boy's dead and we have nothing left to check on in that direction, unless a witness turns up. I keep coming back to Tony. The cartel uses blunt force, maybe you have, but I've never heard of them using finesse."

"I think you're right," said Hatch. "Course there's always a first time for everything, you know. We've got enough to take this to Tony. Read him his rights and see what happens. I know we haven't been out to Noe's place yet, but I can't see that anything out there is going to change anything."

"You're probably right," said Nate. "But I'm still chewing all this around. Tony isn't going anywhere. What do we lose except for a couple of hours by going out to Noe's? I just think we ought not rush this."

"OK.," said Hatch. "You make a point. We'll call it a day and run out there in the morning. But there's still that thing against Tony we've talked about. His small feet. He could have worn Edgar's boots."

"You're right, things are stacking up on Tony."

Chapter 14 – The Clabber Girl House

After talking it over at breakfast the next morning, Nate and Tom decided they would swing by the sheriff's office and speak to the deputy who had found Noe before driving out to his place. Upon their arrival, the dispatcher handed a message to Nate. It was from Mia, asking him to call her. He found an empty desk and placed the call. The call was answered after two rings as though Mia hadn't been very far from her telephone.

Without preamble she said, "I just found something that might be important. The Sheriff brought me boxes of Noe's things – there wasn't much but I was going through the pockets of his jeans, thinking maybe, you know, there might be some money. I didn't find any money, but I found a scrap of wrinkled up paper. I think it was in the jeans he was wearing the last night I saw him. I think maybe it was a note to himself – maybe the woman he worked for. It said '2 hrs. – Romanos' – nothing else."

"Thank you, Mia, this could be important, I really appreciate it," said Nate. "By the way, you know as Noe's widow, you probably inherited his home and land. You could live there if you have to move."

"Yes, Tony tell me that, but I don't think I like to live out there like Noe. I think Tony gonna help me sell the place and Noe's truck. Then I guess I figure out what to do next."

"I wish you the best and thanks again for the information."

"Was *nada,"* said Mia as she hung up.

Nate recited the conversation to Hatch who said, "Looks like Tony's getting deeper involved with Mia, isn't he?"

Hatch took up the city telephone book from behind the desk and quickly found three Romanos listed. "What is that Italian? Didn't know there were any around here."

"Yeah, we got quite a few here in Texas. Lots came in after World War Two. Good people," said Nate.

Meanwhile, Hatch was calling the three listings and on the third call, the lady he spoke to told him that Noe did work for her occasionally. Hatch thanked her and wrote down the address. The two of them went into the dispatcher's office and were told the deputy they were looking for was on patrol. They arranged to meet him at a Mexican food restaurant in his area.

They drove out and met him and bought him an early lunch but gained little information in addition to that which they already possessed. He did confirm that to his knowledge, no one in the vicinity had been questioned. He knew Noe as well as his parents. All were good people. It was a shame Noe just couldn't seem to find his way, etc., etc. They thanked him and returned to their car.

"So, Noe's or Mrs. Romano? Who's next?" asked Hatch.

"I'd like to check out Noe's place and see if there might be any helpful neighbors," said Nate.

Once again following the Sheriff's instructions, the two men drove in silence, each mulling over their thoughts. There was little to no traffic on the county road. The recent rains had dried up, and they left a dust trail in their wake. Hatch every now and then glanced down at the odometer and finally said, "we're getting near if Tony's estimate is close."

On the right side of the road, they passed a double wide with an American flag flying out front. Nate made a mental note to stop there on the way back. They traveled only a short distance further when up ahead they saw the Clabber Girl sign on the roof of a small adobe house. No other houses were in sight. They drove over the cattle guard and up into the dirt driveway. They dismounted and looked at the footprints that were shown in the sheriff's photos. A number in the middle of the trail had a three- or four-inch indention on the right side just as Nate had observed in the photographs. The return tracks were to the right of the original tracks and went through the weeds of the front yard rather than the driveway. They were not distinctive as though the wearer had observed the initial tracks and decided not to duplicate them.

They entered the house, several feet inside they were met by a swarm of flies. There was a wide dark stain, which smelled as though someone had attempted to wash away the blood by dumping water on it. This had not discouraged the flying insects. The two men moved swiftly through the house. It had been emptied of all contents and the foot traffic had destroyed whatever clues there might have once been.

They next checked Noe's truck. As they walked around the front of the house, they could see the remains of old flower beds. At one time lovingly tended, they assumed, by Noe's mother. At each corner of the house there was a large bush with bright green leaves and red fingerlike fruit. That at least was true for the one on the left. The one on the right corner appeared to have had its middle branches stripped of fruit and leaves. Upon closer examination, wrinkled dead leaves lay beneath the tree.

"That's strange," said Hatch, "what would cause that?"

"Only a human," Nate gazed at the mutilated plant. Within seconds, he recalled his first breakfast with Tony. Tony had gone outside and, with his hand, stripped leaves and peppers from a bush growing outside the motel coffee shop door. "Those are chiltepin pepper plants, very popular with the Mexican people. I saw someone harvest the peppers in just that way."

"Who are you talking about?" asked Hatch.

Nate recited the details of the breakfast and how Tony had stressed his fondness for this small red fruit.

"Could be a coincidence, maybe Noe liked them too – this is his house after all," said Hatch. "Whoever took Noe's things must have taken the cooking utensils as well. He had to have some pots and pans, he almost had to have done some cooking way out here." They went back inside and made a minute search of the kitchen and found nothing except some roaches. "I guess we could ask Mia, maybe she might know if Noe cooked and used these peppers. But right now, it seems like another circumstance leading to Tony," said Hatch.

"I think that since we are through here; I want to go talk to the owner of that double wide back down the road," said Nate.

They stopped at the neighbor's dwelling and as they walked up the gravel driveway they were met by a solid looking white man in his late fifties. As they drew together, Hatch flipped open his creds case and said, "FBI, I'm agent Hatch and this is my associate Keller. We'd like to ask you a few questions. We're investigating the death of Noe Floes. Can I have your name?"

"Mueller."

At that, Nate asked, "*Spechen sie Deutsch?*"

"*Ich speche ein bisschen Deutsch.* I was born in Castroville and my folks spoke it among themselves, so I picked up a little, how about you?"

"About the same," said Nate. "I'm going to guess you're retired military."

"That's right, Army; what gave me away?"

"Well, the flag, your haircut, the way you carry yourself, the way you snapped to when Hatch here whipped out his creds."

Mueller replied with a soft chuckle, "You got me. Thirty-year man. Enlisted in '37, nothing going on at home, the depression was still hanging on. Made E-9, and went through two wars, married me a pretty little Mexican girl while I was at Bliss. She inherited these five acres from an uncle so when we retired, we settled here. Nice and quiet, we like it."

Nate said, "Where were you in World War II?

"In '45 I was in Belgium, 101st Airborne."

"My dad was in the 106th."

"Heard them boys got knocked around pretty good," commented Mueller. "You military?"

"Yeah, Nam."

"Boy, that was a real shit hole."

"If I can interrupt," said Hatch, "I assume you heard Noe got killed."

"Yeah, I heard that. Bad thing. He was a nice guy. I had him help me harvest vegetables out of my patch and things. He weren't much for steady work but if he said he'd show up – he'd show up – he might be smelling like an alley behind a bar but he'd show up. I liked the kid."

"I'm sorry I can't be very precise about the date, since we don't have the exact time of death, but thinking back to when you first heard about his death, was there anything strange or unusual that you might have seen or heard prior to that time?"

Mueller thought awhile and then said, “Yeah, there was something – just a few days or so before I heard about his death. It was getting dark, and I was out here feeding my chickens when I thought I heard two gunshots. Well, I thought that’s a little strange – we don’t get no shooting around here except when somebody’s after one of them damn hogs or a snake. So, I didn’t think all that much about it. I finished up with my feeding and stepped out of my hen house and I saw the tail end of a white car driving like hell back toward town. You think maybe I heard the fatal shots?”

“Could be,” Tom Hatch replied. “How about the car, did you get the license plates, make, model, anything else?”

“Nah, white car all I can tell you.”

“See a light bar on top, maybe?”

“Nah, that’s it, sorry.”

“Well, thanks for your help, nice meeting you. Appreciate your service,” said Nate as he and Hatch returned to their vehicle and drove off.

“So, what do you make of that,” said Hatch. “Sheriff’s cars are a light tan, could look white in fading light. Seems like Tony’s our man, things just keep piling up.”

“Looks that way, don’t it?” You wanta swing by and see what Mrs. Romano has to say?”

“Might as well,” replied Hatch.

Chapter 15

The Romano home was a large white Victorian set back from the street with a large well-kept lawn with blooming flowers and bushes around the exterior. The front lawn was shaded by several large oak trees. Their knock was answered within minutes by a small lady with lively eyes and gray hair tucked neatly into a bun.

After stating their business, Tom and Nate were invited in and were led to a living room that could have been the center piece for "Southern Living." After declining an offer of tea or coffee, they took seats on a couch across from a chair chosen by Mrs. Romano.

Hatch was the first to speak. We understand you knew Noe Flores, is that right?"

"Of course, I knew Noe," she said. "He was such a sweet boy. Whenever I could manage to get in touch with him, I would have him do my yardwork. He was a lot better at it than most of the others I had to use when Noe wasn't available. He really was a headache sometimes. Now I don't really want to speak ill of the dead, you know, but it was true. I'm just heart sick over his death. Why in the world would anyone want to hurt such a nice kid? I'm really going to miss him. I kind of depended on him for odd jobs and lawn work ever since my husband passed away."

"We understand, it must have been a real shock," said Hatch. "Do you remember the last time he worked for you?"

"Well, I couldn't tell you the exact date, but Noe did some work for me some time before I heard of his death."

"Anything unusual that day? Did Noe say anything?" said Hatch.

"Well, as I recall, it was very hot. I took a pitcher of iced tea out to Noe. He and I stood in the shade of that big old oak tree out front while he drank several glasses of tea. We just chatted, you know, the weather, the condition of my lawn, that sort of thing. Noe finished drinking and as I walked back to the house, I noticed a white car drive up. I didn't pay it much mind, figured it was someone who wanted to hire Noe."

"Was there anything unusual about the car? Was it white or tan? Could you make out the driver?" asked Nate.

"Could have been tan or beige, as I say, I didn't pay it much mind. I really couldn't see the driver; the sun was reflecting off the windshield. All I could make out was that the driver was small, either a woman or a young person. Whoever it was kinda signaled to Noe to come over. He walked to the driver's side and he and the driver started talking to each other. Wasn't none of my business, so I went on into the house."

"I understand," said Tom Hatch. "How about the car, do you remember the make, license plate number, anything?"

"Young man, I couldn't tell you one car from another if my life depended on it. Sorry, but that's all I can remember. I would like to help catch whoever killed that young man, but I have nothing else."

After thanking her for her time and help, Tom and Nate returned to the car. As they started off, Nate said, "Let's drive over to the newspaper office. I think it's in McAllen, called the *Monitor*."

After a short drive to McAllen and a circle of several downtown blocks, they found the building housing the paper.

As they parked in front of it, Nate said, "I'll be back in a couple of minutes. I've got a hunch."

Hatch raised his eyebrows but remained in the car. In about twenty minutes, Nate returned. "Let's drive out to Edgar's house."

"You want to tell me what's going on?" said Hatch.

"I may be wrong, just bear with me and back me up."

The lady who came to the door in response to their knock was not the woman Tom and Nate had seen in court. Julia McKenzie seemed to have shrunk in size; the black dress she was wearing seemed too large for her. Her hair, which was loose and fell to her shoulders now had even more gray in it. Her eyes were deep in their sockets and rimmed by dark circles. As she opened the door, Tom Hatch attempted to introduce himself and Nate, but he was harshly interrupted.

"I know who you are – what do you want?"

"The Sheriff has asked us to come talk to you about Noe's murder," said Hatch.

"Then it'll be a short conversation 'cause I don't know anything about it."

At that point, Hatch read her her rights and asked if she understood them.

"Of course, I understand them! What I don't understand is why you're going on like this. I don't have anything to say and I don't need a lawyer to tell you that."

"Mrs. McKenzie, may we come in?" Nate interjected. "We do have something to talk to you about and any time you decide to, you can always ask for a lawyer. I really think it would be better if our conversation were held inside."

Julia McKenzie first glared at him almost daring him to go further and then with a soft sigh, she backed away from the door and walked into her living room. She said not a word and did not look back but merely took a seat in an upholstered chair by the fireplace. The room was bright and airy, fitted with tasteful well cared for furniture. Nate and Tom sat on the couch to her left facing the fireplace. It was probably only a minute or two, but it seemed like ten or fifteen before Mrs. McKenzie broke the silence.

"Okay, you've pushed your way into my house – you've rudely intruded into my mourning, so what is this all about?"

"Mrs. McKenzie, we asked the Sheriff to let us do this. We thought it would be much easier on you and much less embarrassing to you if you would just ride with us down to the jail. I don't think you would like to walk out of here in handcuffs alongside a couple of deputies."

"What on earth are you talking about? Jail, handcuffs, are you crazy? Why in the world would I be going to jail?" said Julia, her voice now rising and a hint of fear in her eyes.

"For the murder of Noe Flores," said Nate. "We know you did it and we can prove it." Julia fell back into her chair, while her body seemed to get even smaller. She stared speechless.

"We know you talked to Noe at Mrs. Romano's on the afternoon before his death and promised him money. We suppose you told him it was for the trouble your husband caused him. You took Edgar's gun and boots and drove out to Noe's place and shot him. You struggled to walk in Edgar's boots because they were too large for you. You almost stepped out of them several times and your foot landed on the side of the boot. The indentations in the mud are clearly visible in the photographs the sheriff took. Edgar told us he went to bed early that night and that you went to play bridge. We checked and you were very late to your bridge game which was totally unlike you. You were late because you had driven out to Noe's first."

Julia roused herself to protest, "That's absurd. You're accusing me of murder because I talked to a handyman and because I'm late to a bridge game? I'm gonna sue you for defamation of character. That's what I'm gonna do!"

Unconcerned at this threat, Nate continued by asking Julia if she knew a Mr. Mueller who lived out near Noe. Julia's eyes now worked their way from one to the other as though searching for the significance of this question. Finally, having found no answer, in a small voice, she said, "No, I don't know who he is."

"Well," said Nate, "He knows you, or rather he knows what you look like." With that he took some pictures from the breast pocket of his coat and spread them on the coffee table. There were four portrait type photographs of fiftyish women. One was of Julia McKenzie. "Mr. Mueller lives just east of Noe's place, probably less than a quarter mile. We went out to talk to him the other day. Guess what he told us. The night of Noe's death, he was out in his yard feeding his chickens. He's ex-Army and heard two gunshots. This time of year, he likes to keep track of the white wings, so he keeps his binoculars handy. He's got a real powerful pair he took off a dead German in WW II. Anyway, he steps out in the yard and sees this slight figure sort of stumbling down Noe's muddy driveway to a white Ford. As the Ford starts up on its way to town, the driver is clearly visible. We took these pictures out to him and he, without hesitation, picked out your picture and said that you were the one leaving Noe's place and driving the car. Now Mrs. McKenzie, I can only guess your motive, but motive is not an element of capital murder. We have an eyewitness that places you at the scene at the time of the murder. You had the opportunity to gain and use the murder weapon, as well as the muddy boots. People have been convicted on a lot less than this. Would you like to tell us about it?"

Contrary to her earlier defiance, Julia, now straightened up in her chair and a soft sound, perhaps of relief, escaped her lips before she replied, "I'll never go to prison. That boy over there in Edgar's chair ate at my table for months after Edgar hired him and before he got married. He stopped by just the other day. I'm the next thing to his momma."

"Well, I don't doubt that" observed Tom Hatch, "But that's not part of my job. Do you want to tell us why you did it?"

"Why I did it – that fool Edgar and that little girl. She used to work for me. Edgar would take her home. After a while, I knew something was going on. Didn't like it but kept my mouth shut. I knew Edgar and his lawyer friends would leave me with only the clothes on my back if I divorced him. So, it was painful but, on the surface, life went on and I decided that was the best choice I had. I still had a place in the community. I knew there were rumors – heck, half the fat asses in this town have girls across the river. Some wives know about it and some don't, but we all act like it ain't true. Then that damn fool goes crazy or something and decides to get rid of Noe. Well, it all came out in the trial."

"It's one thing to have your man cheating on you in secret. It's another thing when he's exposed before the whole damn world and made to look like a stupid idiot. I was so humiliated; I could have died. The pain was so real, it was like I cut myself with a knife. I wanted Edgar to hurt like I hurt. I was mad enough at him to kill him but then, I thought, that wouldn't be enough to balance it out. The whole thing just ate at me and then I realized that at the bottom of my problem was Noe. It was really all his fault that things blew up. If he hadn't kept hanging around that girl, Edgar would never have done what he did. So, it came to me, if I got rid of Noe, Edgar would be punished for his stupid attachment to that girl and he would be punished for what he did to me because he'd be blamed for Noe's death. Edgar would sit in prison, constantly in fear for his life. He well knew what happens to law enforcement people in prison. Having been responsible for sending a bunch of guys to prison, Edgar would be in greater danger than most. While he fretted about his safety, I figured he would come to regret everything he'd done. I wanted that. I also figured that sooner or later he would realize what I'd done and he couldn't do one thing about it. That made my plan all the sweeter."

Julia stopped talking, took a deep breath and looked at Tom and Nate with a steady gaze as if to say, *You wanted to hear it, now what?* The silence persisted for some minutes until Tom and Nate realized Julia had said her piece. She had emptied her soul. She was through.

Finally, Nate broke the silence. "Just to clear up a few things. What about the money sent to the funeral home – was that you?"

"Yes," Julia responded without a trace of irony or remorse. "I figured it was the least I could do."

"One more thing," said Nate, "It's a little thing but it is bugging me. Did you strip the peppers off the bird peppers tree to try and frame Tony?"

"I have no idea what you are talking about," said Julia. "What are bird peppers?"

"Well, never mind, it's not important," said Nate. He thought to himself, *I'm still going to wonder about that loose end.*

Hatch then stood up and said to Julia, "Mrs. McKenzie, we need to go downtown, do you need a few minutes to gather your things or make some arrangements?"

"Only my purse, so I can lock my front door. I won't be gone that long," said Julia. With that she walked over to a side table in the hallway, opened up her purse, took out a comb and combed her hair. Then she took out a tissue, moistened it with her tongue and wiped away the dark circles under her eyes. "Damn stuff makes my eyes sting. Don't need it no more – guess I can stop acting like a grieving widow."

Downtown in the jail, with Tony Catalon present, Julia wrote out a full confession and signed it in front of the witnesses. It was hard to gauge Tony's true thoughts about this development. On the one hand, he appeared relieved the true killer had been found and, while he was effusive in his praise of the efforts of Tom Hatch and Nate, yet in his eyes were signs of resentment that his short comings as a law man had been exposed. *Now he wished he had not rushed to conclusions about Edgar, wished he had not patted himself on the back so much and above all, he wished he would have, at least, initiated a minimum routine investigation. He was greatly embarrassed and just a little pissed off at these two guys who had laid bare his mistake.*

However, thinking future cooperation demanded it, and always the politician, Sheriff Tony Catalon said, "If I seemed a little short with you guys, I'm sorry. A lotta stress, you know."

"Sure, we understand," said Nate. "No problem."

Julia, by this time, was back home. The local magistrate had allowed her to sign a personal recognizance bond.

On the way back to their motel, Nate followed Tom as he swung in and parked in front of a low false fronted building whose sign proudly proclaimed, "Turkey Trot Tavern." The establishment had never attained the social prominence its name implied. It was not a tavern; just a Texas beer joint. No one knew why the original owner named it as he had. When he sold to the present owner, the seller didn't tell and the buyer being more frugal than curious didn't ask, since he had no intention of replacing a perfectly good sign.

So it remained over the years and eventually became the iconic watering hole for the neighborhood, a few day laborers out of work, construction workers in the same condition, a thirsty female now and then, and a lot of cowboys. Their presence was announced not so much by their jangling spurs as by the pungent odor which surrounded them. As a matter of pride, they never cleaned the cow dung off their boots. As a consequence, upon entering, one's nostrils were assailed by the odors of stale beer, cigarettes, and the unmistakable hint of a cattle pen.

Five or six tables were occupied as Nate and Tom entered. Conversations stalled as all eyes followed the two suits to the bar as they ordered their beers. Men in suits were an unusual occurrence and required a minute or two of contemplation. Then as on a silent signal, eyes returned front and conversations resumed. Unusual occurrences were not all that unusual to these occupants, sudden death, job loss, divorce, injury on the job were all a painful part of their lives. Two suits merited only a momentary glance.

The bar's interior was lit by neon beer signs around the walls. They shared the space with stuffed deer heads and one cougar. Blue smoke from the many cigarettes hung around the room like a planetary ring at an elevation of three to five feet. A long pitted dark wooden bar ran along one wall and setting on its top were the iconic jars of boiled eggs and pickled pigs feet. A juke box and shuffleboard stood along the opposite wall with tables in between. At the far end, short of the exit and restroom signs, stood a pool table with a metal light fixture dangling from a long cord in the ceiling. The juke box was playing Hank Williams, *Take These Chains from my Heart.*

There were a few early drinkers. The bartender, a slender bald-headed white guy with tats on his arms was bored, standing with his back to the bar watching *Dragnet* reruns on the television. Nate had to raise his voice to get two Lone Stars.

As they were seated, Tom Hatch observed, "You surprised at the handling of Julia?"

"Not really," Nate replied. "You have to know that I'm not unfamiliar with border justice."

"I guess we've both seen some of that," said Hatch. "Now tell me how you knew it was Julia and what made you think you could run such a half-assed bluff?"

"Well, I didn't really know, and I have to admit it was only a hunch. In spite of everything against him, I just couldn't accept that Tony was the killer. That then, only left Julia who had access to both the pistol and the boots. She was a tormented woman; I watched her personality change before my eyes over the eight weeks of trial. It was pure luck, I guess, that she bought my lies about Mueller and the photos. I think guilt played a large part in it. I think at heart, she is a decent person and I suspect it was a huge relief just to get it all out in the open."

"I have to admit, it was one hell of a bluff and, as they say, it's better to be lucky than smart," said Tom Hatch with a smile.

They clinked their bottles and drank deeply. Then Tom ventured, "Have you ever thought of joining the FBI?"

"The FBI? I'm no cop. I'm a lawyer – I try cases. That's what I've always done and that's what I think I'm good at."

"You're good at that all right. but you have a logical and deductive mind. My boss and I both think you'd be a good agent. Besides from what I hear, you are going to have to make a tough decision about your future pretty soon."

"You hear that do you?"

"The FBI knows everything," said Tom with a wide grin. "I don't think you want the top job at the Bar and be an administrator and if you don't take the top job, can you serve under perhaps a lesser man or woman? If not, then what, private practice? You have no clients. Is a law firm going to hire you with your experience and salary expectations and nothing to bring with you?"

"I'm not sure it's as grim as you make out. A good litigator should be able to catch on with somebody. You do make some hard points and I confess they have also been in the back of my mind. Jen and I are getting married soon."

"You don't have to make a decision now, let me know what you decide. If you decide to join, my boss is ready to do everything he can and I have to tell you, the powers that be like him."

"I'll rethink it and talk it over with Jen. No matter what I decide about the job, I hope you and I will stay in touch. I enjoyed working with you."

"I second that," said Tom as they left the bar and headed back to their motel to check out.

Chapter 16 – Shoot-Out on the Highway

The sun was moving toward the western horizon. Tom and Nate packed their belongings and settled up their accounts at the motel. They returned to their vehicles and headed out of town. Just short of turning left onto U.S. 281, Nate glanced into his rear-view mirror and saw Hatch pull into a service station. Instinctively, Nate glanced downward toward his own gas gauge. He had three-fourths of a tank, so he drove on to the highway and headed north for San Antonio.

What he failed to see as he left his motel and drove onto the highway was a large black Lincoln with dark tinted windows. Nate was anxious to get home and see Jen but decided not to push it, so he settled on a comfortable sixty miles an hour. The black car followed but almost at the limits of sight. Had Nate bothered to look in his rear-view mirror, only a black dot would have been visible.

As previously, he passed sun parched land, occasional herds of cattle or goats, some horses, the grass a dusty tan. Small hamlets came and went. There was very little traffic, north or south. There had been a few short-lived showers while he had been in the Valley and now and then there were clumps of wildflowers bravely pushing up through the burned grass along the fence rows. Indian paintbrushes, corn flowers, and brown-eyed Susans struggled to relieve the barren stretches with their colorful assortment. Now and then wooded patches comprising several acres would appear set back from the pastures near the road.

About an hour and a half after leaving Eisenberg and just as he had topped and gone down the far side of a small hill, Nate happened to glance at his side mirror and then at his rear-view mirror, a large black automobile was cresting the small hill and coming toward his rear at high speed. Assuming the car would shortly turn out of his lane to pass him, he wasn't overly concerned. Something about the other automobile's sudden approach and its unseemly speed though prompted Nate to continue observing it. As the two vehicles continued down the highway, the black car was rapidly overtaking him and suddenly Nate realized it intended to ram him.

Without a conscious thought, Nate turned his steering wheel to the right and at about that moment the large black car struck his car a glancing blow. Nate had managed to maneuver his car in the split second before impact just enough to the right so that the on-rushing car struck mainly his left rear bumper. The blow sent his car into a spin, off the roadway and into the roadside ditch. As the black car zoomed past him, there was a burst of gunfire, but no rounds struck Nate or his car. Apparently, the impact had thrown off the shooter's aim.

Nate had immediately thrown his gear shift into neutral and he was now heading backward, he fought the wheel and pumped gently on his brakes. Fortunately, since there was very little rainfall in this part of the state the roadside ditches existed more in name than in reality. As it was, Nate managed to control his car without it turning over. As soon as it began to slow, he pushed his gear shift into low and pulled up out of the ditch onto the highway heading south. He shifted into high gear and rammed his foot down hard on the accelerator, the BMW responded like a trained mare calf roper. It shot down the pavement. Nate glanced in his mirror and saw the Lincoln turning around. As he moved south once again, Nate realized that as fast as his car was, it was no match on a straight-a-way with the obviously super charged pursuer.

A plan began to form in Nate's mind. It was dangerous and crazy, but it offered hope. There was none in a race down the highway. Soon a wooded area appeared to Nate's right. There was pastureland near the road but fifty yards or so to the rear was woodland – or at least what passed for such in South Texas.

Nate took a deep breath, cut his wheel sharply and headed for a fence post. He hit the fence post square on snapping it off at the ground level and laying down the barbed-wire fence which his wheels easily passed over. Nate didn't look back, he headed for the trees which, as he had seen very briefly from the road, were not densely packed but spread out. On he went, slowing somewhat and steering around live oaks, elms, mesquites, and cedar trees, crushing over or into prickly pear cactus, huisache, cenizo, occasional mountain laurels, and desert ironwood. Branches, dirt, leaves, twigs, and vines were crashing into his car. The noise inside the car sounded like baseballs hitting it. *If I get out of this*, he thought, *I'll sure need a new paint job*. He had no time for thoughts, however. As one tree after another suddenly loomed up in front of him. All he could do was steer, down shift, brake, upshift, accelerate, and continue heading in a direction he hoped would eventually intersect the highway again.

Meanwhile, his pursuers were having the difficulties Nate had wished for. The large heavy Lincoln was not nearly as nimble as the BMW. It had to greatly reduce its speed and often times had to find alternate routes since its turning radius was greater than Nate's. As it moved further into the woods, the ground became softer as the shade of the trees had prevented the ground from fully drying out from the recent showers. As the big car cut in and out of the trees, ruts began to appear, and its rear wheels began to spin. Finally, after a particularly sharp cut, the rear wheels lost traction and, as the driver applied more gas, the rear wheels dug a pit and forward progress stopped.

Nate caught a glance in his mirror of two men jumping out of the Lincoln evidently to push. This was the chance Nate was waiting for. He steered out of the woods as soon as he could, drove through a fence, up out of the ditch, and onto the highway with his foot pressing the accelerator to the floorboard and heading south to civilization.

After several miles, Nate caught sight of an approaching car. It was Tom's Ford. Nate slowed and waved his arm. Tom recognized him and slowed and stopped at the center line. Nate stopped opposite. Side by side now Nate waved off Hatch's questions and shouted, "There's some crazy bastards in a black Lincoln trying to kill me. They're stuck off the road right now, but they'll be here in a few minutes. I can't outrun them."

"A black Lincoln, eh? I'll bet that's the same car I saw when I stopped for gas. A big black Lincoln with tinted windows seemed out of place for this part of the country so, on an impulse, I called in the plates. Sure, enough they were stolen. Had to be cartel guys," said Hatch.

"Oh, my God!" Nate swore briefly. "Jen! I gotta get home."

"Way ahead of you, partner," Tom Hatch replied. "When I couldn't keep up with those guys, I called DPS highway patrol, all the local sheriff offices along 281 and my boss. Everyone is scrambling to get help headed our way. My boss, recognizing the possibility of a cartel retaliation attempt, has ordered agents to both our homes so Jen's safe."

"Thank God," said Nate. "They must have it in for us for taking out their boy. They must have missed you when you stopped to get gas."

"Yeah, guess I lucked out and so did everyone at the service station. Those people are nuts. They have their code against informers and this eye for an eye thing. They have to revenge their guys. We gotta deal with it. Pull your car across the road, we'll set up a roadblock."

"Are you crazy?" asked Nate. "That car those bastards are driving is up armored – it's a damn tank. Plus, they have submachine guns."

"Help is on the way," said Hatch, as he fingered his radio microphone. "All we are going to do is delay them – maybe the calvary gets here before they do."

"Tom, I going to tell you, I do not share your faith that the good guys always win over the bad guys. But, as I'm short of ideas at the moment, I guess your plan is the best we have. I know we can't outrun them. That car they're driving can outrun either one of ours. So, I guess we have no choice but to make a stand. Got a spot picked out for us to set up?"

Tom Hatch surveyed the tabletop landscape. He looked to his rear and saw that the only rise in sight was the small hill he had just passed over. The same one that Nate had first spotted the Lincoln topping in his side mirror. "We'll sit up our block thirty or forty yards on the far side of that little hill," he said pointing. "You go on ahead and I'll turn around and join you."

So, that's what they did. Nate pulled forward over the hill and parked headed west across the north bound lane. Hatch drove up and parked his car in line with Nate's blocking the south bound lane. Both hurried out of their cars. Hatch waved to Nate as he opened the trunk of his car. He extracted a Remington 870 twelve-gauge pump shotgun and tossed it to Nate along with a box of shells. "That's not plugged and has an extended magazine tube, you can put seven in the mag and one in the chamber. That's a twenty-inch barrel with double-ought-shot, so your effective range is probably forty yards or maybe a little more."

"Thanks for the info. I'm supposed to go macho man-to-man with buck shot against an AK-47?"

"Sorry pal, the FBI doesn't give us AKs," said Hatch.

Both men took cover at each end of the line, expecting the Lincoln to try to burst through the center gap. They had waited only a few minutes when they heard the roar of a powerful engine and suddenly a black hulk appeared at the top of the rise. Instead of bursting the line, the Lincoln swerved into the right-hand ditch, hardly slowing. It bounced and rocked side to side but the driver brought it under control and in seconds it had flashed by the makeshift road block and had bounced onto the highway, skidded into a partial left turn and came to rest thirty or forty yards from the block in the center of the pavement. Nate and Tom scuttled to get to the other side of their cars as the occupants of the Lincoln opened their doors but remained standing behind them as they took aim and began firing their weapons. Both passengers were armed with AK-47's and both gunmen let out long bursts that blew out all windows of both cars and racked the bodies with bullet holes. Hatch and Nate were crouched behind the rear wheels of their respective autos.

"No fire discipline," shouted Nate.

"Maybe not, but a lucky dumbass can still kill you," Hatch shouted back.

Nate went down on his stomach and crawled to his front wheel where he had a line of sight and then cautiously poked the Remington around his front tire. The lower legs of the front seat passenger and the driver were visible beneath the car doors. Nate let off a round at the legs of the gunner at the front passenger door. Before the echo of his first round had dissipated, he pumped and fired another round. There was a scream and his target fell to the ground dropping his weapon and grabbing his lower legs as blood seeped between his fingers. His curses now replaced his screams of pain as he grabbed his weapon. His curses were suddenly stilled as Hatch fired three rounds into his now exposed body. Sensing their vulnerability, the two remaining gunmen scuttled quickly. The driver ducked back behind the Lincoln and gave covering fire to his companion who took off running to the rear with the Lincoln between himself and Nate and Hatch. At about twenty yards to the rear of the Lincoln, the gunmen started to move toward the ditch on the left-hand side. Both Tom and Nate fired their weapons at him causing him to duck back in line with the Lincoln.

"He's trying to flank us," said Tom, "And pretty soon he's going to realize he's out of our range. Here; trade guns, I'll take the Remington and try to ambush him before he gets to our rear."

"Ambush him? What're you going to hide behind out there in that field. There isn't nothing there but grass stubble and that damn gun of his can reach out about four hundred yards. You won't be able to even get close to him," said Nate.

"Well, we have to do something and do it fast. We're sitting ducks," said Tom. "Got any ideas?"

"I've been thinking – if we could get to that AK-47 laying out there on the ground, we might have a chance."

"Maybe, but how are we going to get it? That guy behind the car isn't shooting a BB gun," said Tom.

"Here's the deal. The guy behind the Lincoln has to move from side to side to fire. He can't see or shoot at us from behind the car. Say we force him behind the car and keep him there. I could crawl under my car to the Lincoln, go under it to the left door and crawl out and get the AK – probably shoot out the guy's legs as soon as I get my hands on the AK," said Nate.

"Might work," said Tom, "but I'm the one doing the crawling. You cover me."

"Oh, no, it was my plan."

"You're a civilian, I'm a cop. That's my job."

"I'm a civilian getting my ass shot off," said Nate. "That's enough authority for me."

"We don't have time for debate," said Tom. "Cover me."

He was on his hands and knees as bullets from the gunmen struck the Ford in a violent fusillade. It was as if their opponent had anticipated their plan and was determined to thwart it.

Chapter 17 – To the Rescue

About then Jesus Valdez was driving north on highway 281. Jesus was not only a happy man, he was a contented one. He was 48 years old and had been married to the same woman for 28 years. They had four daughters and a son – his pride and joy. His oldest daughter was in her second year of college in Eisenberg, the second oldest was a senior in high school, the twins were in the tenth grade and his son in the eighth. All were doing well.

Jesus and his wife had worked hard and saved their money and bought a small house, nothing fancy but it had electricity and city utilities. Luxuries he never had growing up in Mexico. His parents brought him to Texas when he was ten. He wife and children had all been born in Texas and were American citizens. One day Jesus wanted to become one too. Now though he had to make a living.

He had started his hauling business ten years ago. He would haul anything he could fit on his truck. He could fit it up as a stake bed and haul goats and pigs. Damn he hated pigs. He and his brother-in-law kept the old truck running. He had wanted to repair his brakes, but this job came up and he needed the money. He knew he was losing brake fluid and his truck turned to the left and made a grinding sound when he applied the brakes. But San Antonio was a straight run, not a lot of traffic in between there and McAllen so he figured he would be okay.

He had managed to roll a Bull Durham while holding the steering wheel of his truck with his knees. Presently he was trying to strike a kitchen match on the rusty dashboard. He was leaning forward and to his right over the steering wheel with his hand rolled between his lips and his eyes on the match.

He was driving a 1959 GMC flat bed with a load of live chickens in crates stacked five high, four wide and eight deep and they smelled. However, they smelled to others, they smelled like money to Jesus. He would be paid for the trip as soon as he delivered them in San Antonio. A long way to go but plenty of time to get there so he was lazing along at around fifty.

The match head broke off, he cursed and reached for the glove compartment for another match. Just as he got his fingers on one and was preparing to straighten up, he saw a huge black car squarely in the center of the highway and now right in front of him. He let out a curse and jammed his foot on the brakes. The old truck did not respond all that quickly. He wished he had given it the brake job it needed. Jesus was now praying as he stood on the brakes. Instead of stopping the old truck, they locked, and the truck began to skid. Jesus tried to get both hands on the wheel, but it was too late, the wheel was jerked out of his hands as the truck turned sideways and continued to skid while it began to sway side to side and threatened to turn over.

Fortunately, for Jesus, but less so for the gunman behind the Lincoln, the truck remained upright as it rammed into the rear of the Lincoln and crushed the driver of the car crouching there. The impact caused eight or nine crates to be thrown from the truck. They shattered on impact with the ground releasing their contents. The dazed chickens tumbled out and were soon wandering about underfoot, waving their clipped wings, cackling with indignation and, of course, defecating. The air was filled with dust, smoke, and chicken feathers. The smell of burnt rubber, gasoline, cordite, and chicken shit assailed the senses and burned the eyes as Nate and Hatch slowly moved around the right side of the black car, keeping it between them and the armed man in the field.

The crumpled body of the driver lay in a bloody pile, no longer recognizable as human, on the ground between the two vehicles. The truck would have to be moved before access to the body could be gained.

Neither Nate nor Hatch had seen anything of the driver of the truck. Nate became concerned and rushed around the truck and jerked open the passenger door. The first thing he noticed was a large straw hat moving back and forth on the truck floorboards. At the same time there arose a string of Spanish words which Nate assumed to be curses as on closer inspection he saw a thin man in dirty overalls moving back and forth on the floorboards.

Nate leaned into the doorway and shouted, “Are you all right?” The straw hat tilted backward, and a brown whiskered face appeared.

“*Si,* I’m okay but my truck she is wrecked, my chickens are running the hell all over and I can’t find my got damn cigarette that I spent the last ten miles rolling and you ask if I am all right?”

“Sorry, about that, I meant are you hurt?”

“I don’t think so,” Jesus slowly pulled himself up and climbed out of the truck. He swayed as his feet touched the ground, but he grabbed hold of the truck to steady himself and he was soon able to stand on his own. “What in the hell is going on here?”

As Hatch undertook an explanation, the sounds of sirens split the air and shortly two DPS highway black and white patrol cars from opposite directions slid to stops on either side of the wreck. After a brief conference with Hatch, the troopers returned to their patrol cars and began throwing flares out on the highway. They then took up positions fifty or sixty yards down the road in both directions to head off traffic. At the sound of the sirens the gunman ran for the woods. Within a short while a tan Ford pickup with a whip antenna drove up. Both doors displayed a star and the words Buchel County Sheriff Department.

The man who exited the truck could have been a character in a western movie. He was over six feet, wiry, wind burnt, wearing scuffed boots, wrinkled jeans, and a brown shirt with a badge on his left breast. His face was thin with a white mustache above his upper lip and he had deep wrinkles around his eyes from squinting in the sun. He wore a holstered revolver low on his right hip held up by a wide belt lined with cartridges. He walked up to Hatch and Nate with his right hand extended, and with what might have passed as a smile on his mouth.

"I'm Buck Newsom, the sheriff hereabouts."

"I'm special agent Tom Hatch and this is Nate Keller." said Hatch, making the introductions. "Sure, glad to see you."

"Looks like you boys got yourselves a little gun play...put down a couple bad ones here. Good work, my boys will take it from here."

"You're more than welcome to it," Tom Hatch answered, with deep feeling. "The remaining gunsel took off toward the woods over there when he heard the sirens."

Looking in the direction indicated by Hatch, Newson said, "Them woods ain't very deep, but Mr. Yepes has a big stock tank behind them trees. It's got high banks; my guess is your man will end up there."

As he spoke these words, a pickup identical to his pulling a double horse trailer pulled up. The Sheriff walked over and shortly the pickup was off the road and the deputies were saddling their horses. “Now when you all cut that fence, remember to leave a little wire on the end to tie to when we’re done here. We don’t want Mr. Yepes to lose no cattle ‘cause of us.”

The deputies waved and lead their horses down to the barbed-wire fence. One produced a wire cutter and soon both were mounted and moving away toward the trees.

“Sheriff,” said Nate, “your deputies are going after a crazy man with a submachine gun and they’re packing lever action Winchesters. I mean that gun might have won the West but it’s no match with an AK-47.”

“Don’t you worry ‘bout that,” replied Sheriff Newsom. “Them boys can shoot the eye out of a cottontail at a hundred yards – on horseback – at a gallop.” He didn’t crack a smile as he looked up to the sky.

Nate’s attention was now drawn to the sky also and the sudden arrival of a helicopter. As soon as it settled, James White sprang out followed by four more FBI agents, all carrying automatic weapons. White and Hatch conferred, White walked back to the helicopter, gave a few instructions and it became airborne. As it rose, Nate could see an agent taking a seat in the open doorway with a long gun, with a scope, across his knees.

As White walked back to the wreck, he was attacked by an irate chicken and in his attempt to elude his attacker, White stepped into some chicken mess. “God damnit! Somebody get these damn chickens out of here, you can’t even hear yourself think. Smitty, you and McGraw help this man get them damn birds."

As Jesus and the two agents began chasing the chickens, the noise level accelerated. In the midst of all this, a Border Patrol carry-all drove up. A sergeant came over to the group and after being given the particulars rejoined his men. The carry-all drove through the fence and stopped at the edge of the woods. The men dismounted, they were all armed with long guns and after a brief conference they spread out and entered the woods along with two FBI agents.

Nate turned to Hatch, “Where are the Marines? Man, you got everyone else out here.”

“They’re probably on their way,” deadpanned Hatch.

There were sounds of an automatic weapon, several rifle shots from the helicopter and then only the sound of the copter.

The men at the wreck watched the horizon and made small talk. White lit a cigarette. Sheriff Newsom added a pinch of Redman to his cheek. Meanwhile, Jesus and the two FBI agents had corralled most of the roving chickens, except for a few who had really “flown the coop!” With baling wire supplied by Jesus, they had managed to repair some of the broken crates and fill them with chickens. The chickens left from the nonrepairable crates were stuffed into existing crates amid a rising clamor of chicken discontent.

Suddenly out of the woods came the deputies on horseback with the other gunman in their van with his hands cuffed behind his back. Shortly the Border Patrol and FBI agents emerged also and formed around the trio. As the group neared the fence line, the helicopter landed on the roadway. White and the sheriff walked over briefly to speak to the crew and then down to the fence line where White took charge of the prisoner. There were no objections. The prisoner, White, and the FBI agents boarded the copter and within minutes they were airborne and out of sight.

A convoy of a single ambulance, three wreckers, and an old Volkswagen van with the hand-painted slogan BUCHEL SHERIFF AUXILIARY on the side pulled up. These were followed shortly by a yellow Texas Highway Department stake bed truck. Jesus having given his statement, was permitted to continue on his way. The DPS patrolmen cautioned him to stay under fifty because of his bad brakes and he was forced to promise to have them repaired in San Antonio. One wrecker hooked up to the Lincoln and took it away to the FBI office in San Antonio. The other wreckers hooked up to Nate's and Hatch's cars. Nate and Hatch rode in the lead wrecker.

Before they left, the large lady driving the van jumped out, set up a folding table in the ditch, and a coffee urn.

Sheriff Newsom explained, "That's Molly, she has a police scanner and shows up everywhere, she won't listen to nothin' I say. Makes pretty good coffee though and I bet she bought all the doughnuts the local bakery had."

Even as he was speaking the deputies and Border Patrol men, now relieved of their prisoner were crowding the table and laughing and talking. As Nate and Hatch sped away, they looked back and saw the DPS troopers and highway workmen join the group. The flares had been picked up and the traffic, as it was, had begun to flow again.

"Looks like a party," Tom Hatch observed with a sigh, "Wish I'd grabbed a coupled of those doughnuts."

"Me too," replied Nate. "Getting shot at always makes me hungry."

Both men were silent, lost in their thoughts, on the ride back to San Antonio. The wrecker dropped them off at the FBI building and once inside they were bombarded with questions which only ceased when James White entered the room. He had both Tom and Nate join him in his conference room. He had each of them recite their part in the afternoon chase. They each then had to write out and sign a written statement of the events.

White congratulated the both of them and reassured Nate that he would face no legal jeopardy. Hatch was told to check out a car and take a few days off. Nate was told White's office would handle the claim for his car. So finally, Nate was free to check out a government car and head to Austin.

Chapter 18 – A Peaceful Interlude

As Nate, weary and bedraggled, approached home late that night he saw a white Chevrolet parked at the curb in front of his house. As he drove his government loaner up onto his driveway, the Chevy's interior lights came on as two navy blue suits emerged from the now open doors. Nate came to a stop, killed the engine, and opened the driver's side door but before he could exit, the nearest suit yelled, "FBI, keep your hands in sight!"

"I live here," responded Nate. "Thanks for your help but the danger is over, radio your headquarters."

"We'll need to see some ID. Very slowly produce your wallet," said the nearest agent.

About that time, the front door banged as it was flung open, and Jen shot out of the door and down the front steps. She was barefoot wearing short shorts and a tee shirt. Her hair was in a ponytail and flying in the wind as she raced across the lawn shouting,

"Nate, Nate, oh my God are you okay? I was so worried."

By now Nate was out of the car and could do nothing but watch as the blond apparition launched herself at him. Jen had both arms around his neck, both legs around his waist and was bombarding his face with kisses.

"Looks like he belongs here," one of the agents said drily to the other.

"I think you're right. Let's get out of here."

Neither Nate nor Jen noticed as they retreated to their car and drove away.

"You're sure you are all right?" asked Jen as they finally made it inside the house. "Can I fix you something to eat – I'll bet you're hungry."

"No, I'm fine," said Nate, "just need a shower."

"Of course," said Jen. "Oh Nate, I'm so glad you are home and all in one piece."

"Me too," said Nate kissing her again. They walked arm in arm to the bathroom. Jen pushed the curtain aside, leaned over the tub and turned on the water. Nate had, in the meantime, stripped off his clothing and stepped into the tub and into the stream of water. He began soaping himself when the end of the curtain was suddenly thrust aside, and a naked Jen stepped into the tub.

"Like some company?" Nate reached for her. He was no longer tired. They moved together and it was like the first time. Their movements dislodged the shower curtain which fell to the floor while water sprayed the bathroom floor. Neither noticed as they contrived to make love in the tub with the shower pouring down on them.

Nate slept late the next morning. Jen had already left for work but left an affectionate note on the breakfast table for Nate. Nate choked down a cup of warmed up coffee, got dressed and drove to the State Bar Law Center.

"Hi Nickey." said Nate to the attractive receptionist.

"Hello, stranger – I hear you've turned cowboy."

"Don't believe everything you hear."

Settled in behind his desk, Nate began returning telephone calls and reading his mail. By one thirty, Nate had more or less caught up and he realized he'd missed lunch. He took the elevator down to the first-floor and walked next door to the Texas Chili Parlor. There he was joined by several attorneys from the office and, in spite of his protestations, was prevailed upon to give an edited version of his recent escapade.

Jen met him at the door as he returned home. A welcome home kiss soon turned into something else so they found themselves preparing and eating a late dinner. For the next several weeks this became their daily routine. Eventually, as is the usual case, their lives became more prosaic. As they were having dinner one evening, Jen brought up the subject of marriage.

"You know Nate, you asked me to marry you and I said I would. If you still feel that way, I would like to start planning."

"Of course, I still feel that way," said Nate. "We've been a little busy and I'm sorry so much time has gone by but I'm all for getting it done."

Jen took a few days off and went to visit her parents in Dallas. When she returned in a week, she had purchased her dress, a date and time had been firmed up as had a venue for the post wedding party. As they discussed the matter, a small problem arose. Jen planned on four bridesmaids, but Nate said he didn't know four men to stand up with him.

"I guess I could ask Tom and Jonas, but after that I draw a blank."

"You really cannot think of two other guys?"

"No, I really can't. I don't have any relatives that I know of. You know I'm a private person – sort of sufficient unto myself, I guess. So, I just never made an effort to cultivate friends – I mean I know a bunch of people to speak to but none of them are close."

"That's kind of sad," said Jen.

"Not really," said Nate, "I've never missed having friends and besides when I met you, I increased my friends by one hundred percent."

To resolve it, two of Jen's friends decided to help with the post wedding party. Whether by flipping a coin, drawing cards, or some method practiced only by the female of the species, Nate didn't know how Jen accomplished this – and he never asked.

Six weeks later they were duly married and then flew to Hawaii for their honeymoon. In between making love at least twice a day, they managed to do all the tourist things. Nate got a mild sunburn because he thought it unmanly to smear himself with sunscreen. They were amazed at the taste of fresh pineapples. Nate had a momentary pushing match with a Japanese man at the Arizona memorial. All in all, after a week they were exhausted and looking forward to Austin and rest.

Back at his day job several weeks later, Nate received a telephone call from Tom.

"Hey man, what's up?" said Nate as he answered the phone.

"Thought, I'd bring you up to date on things," said Hatch

"Great, I've been wondering."

"You remember that captured gunman? Well, even though he was pretty low in the pecking order, he's proven to be really helpful. He overheard and saw and remembered a bunch of stuff. He was pretty smart. His disclosures have led to the rolling up of most of El Tigre's operation in South Texas. El Tigre himself tried to run to Mexico but was identified and detained at the border crossing at Eagle Pass."

"That's great news," said Nate.

"Yeah, there's more," Tom Hatch continued. "It seems that El Tigre had disguised himself as an old woman. He arrived at the Border Patrol station in an old rusted and beat up 1962 Chevrolet pickup with two of his henchmen dressed up as field hands. I talked to the Border Patrol agent who made the arrest. The agent said he looked in the passenger side window of the truck and immediately got suspicious, he said, "I couldn't believe a benevolent God woulda ever made a woman that ugly – by that time of day she had a real bad five o'clock shadow. I had a drug dog walk the car and it alerted at the driver's door. So, I had all the occupants dismount and submit to a search. It didn't take the female agent long to discover that the woman she was searching wasn't a woman. The dumb ass driver had a baggie in his boot." Hatch then personally resumed the narrative. "They were all turned over to the FBI and they, along with El Tigre, who turned out to be one Emilo Zuma, are awaiting trial in the U.S. District Court in Brownsville."

"Well, guess that puts a ribbon on it then," said Nate. "Quite an experience for a weary trial lawyer."

"Not quiet," said Tom. "You still haven't committed to us."

"The FBI?"

"Who else?"

"Well, I did get a nice letter and an offer from your boss," said Nate. "I'm still thinking on it."

Chapter 19 – Jailbreak

It was an unusually warm and humid morning in South Texas even for mid-September. A low-pressure area had hovered overhead for several days bringing welcome rain. Overhead it was cloudy with a fine mist falling and a forecast of heavier moisture to follow during the rest of the day.

Henry Singleton maneuvered his aging prison bus into the designated loading area in the rear of the Cameron County jail where he was met by two federal marshals. The U.S. Attorney's Office in Brownsville had no jail of its own so it contracted with the county to house federal prisoners awaiting trial or waiting to be transported to federal prisons after conviction. This morning Henry had been assigned to provide transport for six federal prisoners from the county jail to the federal courthouse less than two miles away.

As he sat in the bus waiting for the marshals to bring the day's contingent of prisoners aboard, he lit his third cigarette of the morning and coughed as he drew the smoke deeply into his lungs. He brushed tears from his eyes and hoped his old bus would make it through the day without breaking down. The bus and the fleet of which it was a component was owned by the brother-in-law of the local congressman so no matter how many requests the U.S. Attorney and marshals made, they were not going to get their own transport. So, while the job wasn't that much of a job, at least, Henry felt his job was safe so long as the congressman got re-elected. He did wish though his boss would spend a little more on maintenance and most of all, he wished for air conditioning.

At that moment, there was a banging on the door and Henry was roused from his reverie. One of the marshals was standing just outside at the head of a line of six prisoners shackled together. Henry hurriedly opened the door, and the chained men began to pass by him and into the interior of the bus. Henry had no way of knowing that one of these men was known in certain circles as El Tigre.

Henry was less than average height, in his mid-fifties and unmarried. His one obsession in life was soccer. Well, not exactly as he had to admit to himself. It wasn't soccer, it was betting on soccer and in off season betting on anything and everything, even reruns of soccer games. Henry was not a very good gambler and while he occasionally won, by and large his habit kept him broke so that he lived from pay day to pay day. Among his less socially acceptable idiosyncrasies was his failure to bathe or wash his clothes with any degree of regularity. Today he wore a pair of battered athletic shoes, no socks, cut-off jeans, and a short-sleeved shirt with the name of his employer on the left breast and across the back.

The bus itself, while showing its age, had a unique interior design. The first two rows of seats had been removed creating a space for a guard to sit directly behind the driver and facing the bus interior. This space was secured by an accordion steel door controlled by the driver who also controlled the rear exit door. The guard's space had windows on either side which were not barred, as were those in the rear of the bus.

The marshals got the prisoners seated and ran the common chain through eyelets welded aisle side to each seat. As usual there was a lot of noise, most of it profanity directed toward the marshals. Eventually things settled down with all prisoners in place. Front to back, they were El Tigre, three of his minions, a bank robber, and an overweight middle-aged man with a bad comb over accused of being a pedophile. The marshals closed and locked the accordion gate and then one took the guard's seat while the other retreated to their government Ford and drove it up behind the bus. The convoy started off. Traffic was light and everything seemed routine until the bus reached the edge of Gladys Porter Zoo.

It was then Henry happened to glance at his sideview mirror. He saw a black motorcycle with two black clad figures on board coming at speed zigzagging through traffic. "Crazy fool," Henry thought out loud. In a matter of seconds, the cycle was alongside the bus and the pillion rider rose upright and produced an Uzi submachine gun. The rider pointed his weapon at the open window of the bus where the marshal was seated. He let off a short burst striking the marshal's head and shoulders. The unfortunate officer was dead before he even realized the threat. With a burst of speed, the cycle and its riders were out of sight in the blink of an eye.

As this was happening, a large garbage truck pulled out of the intersection in front of the bus completely blocking its forward progress. Behind the bus, the cab of an eighteen-wheeler viciously drove into the rear of the trailing marshal's automobiles driving it forward into the rear of the bus. Its air bag deployed leaving the battered officer completely helpless.

Masked men armed with submachine guns jumped from the truck cab and the garbage truck and ran for the door of the bus which had now come to a stop.

Henry, along with the prisoners, was thrown about but his seat belt prevented any serious injury. The bus, of course, had no air bag so all Henry had to do to free himself was release the seat belt. This he did as soon as he regained his breath. He didn't stop to question why he hadn't been killed. He rolled out of his seat, hit the toggle switch to unlock the rear door and began crawling on his hands and knees down the center aisle toward the rear of the bus just as fast as he could. The prisoners had been thrown about and their dazed condition, as well as their chain, prevented any of them from impeding Henry's progress. So, while the armed and masked men were rushing to the front of the bus, Henry was doggedly heading in the opposite direction. As he neared the rear of the bus, he could hear the sounds of blows against the door of the bus. He prayed that it would hold for a few seconds more. It did and Henry tumbled out of the rear of the bus and as he landed, he crawled immediately beneath the marshal's wrecked Ford. He lay there trying to catch his breath and praying none of the armed men would start looking for the bus driver.

The bus door was finally forced open. Two men entered: one armed with a submachine gun, the other with a bolt cutter. The other two took up positions around the bus. Inside, the man with the bolt cutter first cut the shackles off Zuma and handed him an automatic pistol. As Zuma made his way to the front of the bus, the chains were being removed from his men who quickly followed him down the bus aisle.

The remaining two prisoners were clamoring to be released also. The black clad man with the bolt cutter handed it to the bank robber. He then drew an automatic pistol from the holster strapped to his right leg and calmly shot the pedophile in his face. He then ran down the aisle and joined his comrades just as a white panel truck drove up. Everyone quickly jumped on board and the truck took off as sirens began to sound. The attack lasted less than five minutes. The panel truck was later found abandoned at the Brownsville airport parking lot. Upon being questioned by the police, none of the employees knew anything and hadn't seen anything.

The police surmised that El Tigre's people had stashed one or more vehicles there. The airport cameras revealed a lot of coming and going, including the white panel truck entering the airport parking lot. Once in the lot among hundreds of vehicles, the cameras lost it.

El Tigre was in the wind.

Chapter 20 – The Cartel Retaliates

Four or five weeks after returning home, Nate received a telephone call from Hatch.

"Nate, I've got bad news."

"What is it?"

"Emilo Zuma has escaped while he was being transported to the federal courthouse."

It took Nate a few moments to digest this information, finally he said, "You mean El Tigre is no longer in custody? When and how did this happen?"

Hatch said, "About two hours ago." He went on to explain what he knew about the escape and further that at this time no one had a clue as to El Tigre's whereabouts. "Nate, this puts you and Jen in danger. I'm calling the Austin office to send a car over to keep watch."

"I don't know that's necessary," said Nate. "He doesn't know where I live and besides, right now he's more worried about staying out of the reach of the law than anything else. He's also got to rebuild his organization and square himself with the big cartel bosses, so I don't think there's much danger. But Jen and I will be careful."

"You sure about this?" asked Hatch. "You know that's what we are here for – it's not like you are putting us out."

"I know," said Nate. "Thanks for offering. Take care of yourself." He hung up the phone.

Nate told Jen about Tom's call and reassured her that there was no cause for alarm but that they probably needed to be a little more careful. Jen promised to lock all the doors when she was home alone. In addition, Nate purchased a 92FS Beretta for Jen and they spent hours the next several weekends at a shooting range. Jen had a good eye and in the several weekends became quite proficient with the semi-automatic.

On these occasions, Nate removed a shoe box from the top shelf of the master bedroom closet and removed his .45 Browning semi-automatic pistol he had carried in Nam. After the first weekend of firing with Jen, he was pleased to note that he had lost none of his skill.

Being thus reassured that they had done what they could to prepare for an attack, both Jen and Nate's concerns over the coming weeks passed onto other matters. That all changed in a matter of minutes when several weeks later, on returning home from work, Nate noticed the front door was ajar. In point of fact, it looked like it had been smashed in. With a premonition of something being terribly wrong, Nate sprang out of his car even before it had come to a complete stop and raced for the front door. He entered the house calling out Jen's name. There was no answer. He went from room to room – no Jen. In the master bedroom he found Cat lying on the carpet bleeding from what appeared to be the crease of a bullet across his right shoulder.

The house was in disarray, furniture knocked over, the telephone pulled from the wall in the kitchen, lamps overturned, and paper and books scattered around about. He rushed back to the bedroom and while the telephone there had been knocked off the bedside table, it still worked. He called 911 and then the vet clinic where Jen worked and was relieved when he was assured Cat would be picked up and taken care of.

His next call was to the FBI office in San Antonio and was lucky to catch Hatch who was at his desk working late as usual.

"Hey, Nate, what's up?"

With a touch of hysteria in his voice, Nate answered, "Tom, they've taken her!"

"What? Who? Calm down and tell me what's going on." Between sobs and gasps for air, Nate managed to describe his homecoming. "You know who's behind it, don't you? If he lays one finger on Jen, I'm going to kill that worthless piece of shit. Screw that, I'm going to kill him anyway," said Nate.

"Nate! Nate! Calm down. I promise you we'll get her back. You're one of us and that means an all-out effort – no stone unturned but you have to get a hold of yourself. Coming unglued isn't helping anything."

After several deep breaths, Nate agreed. In response to Tom's question, he told him there was a large vacant commercial lot on the corner about three houses down.

"Okay, said Tom, "I've put out an A.P.B. and ordered up the helicopter, I'll see you within the hour."

Noise at the front door alerted Nate to the arrival of the Austin police. A large man dressed in boots and jeans with a badge and pistol on his belt strode into the room and introduced himself as Detective Sergeant Baily.

Nate introduced himself and Baily, while moving his head from side to side said, "You got a hell of a mess here. Wanna tell me about it?" So, Nate did. While he was doing so, other detectives were moving about checking for fingerprints and taking pictures.

All at once from the kitchen came an exclamation. "Mother of God – Christ almighty!" A very young detective brushed pass to end upon his knees in the front lawn throwing up.

"What the hell?" demanded Detective Sergeant Baily as he moved to the kitchen. There on the counter in a plastic grocery bag now pulled down was a bloody severed head. Baily gasped and struggled not to lose his own dinner. "Great shit, where did that come from?"

Nate standing behind him, swallowed a few times and after the bile allowed him to speak said, "I know who that is and where it came from."

"Better start talking," Baily advised, his eyes narrowing.

So, Nate did; relating the story of the fire in Bayon County, shooting the cartel gunman and the shoot-out on the highway.

"The head belongs to the gunman captured out on the highway. He made a deal with the Feds and ratted out El Tigre, I guess you've heard of him?"

"Oh, yeah," said Baily.

"Anyway," Nate continued, "His information was very vital and led to the arrest of El Tigre and the destruction of most of his network. The guy was put in witness protection, but it looks like El Tigre found him after all."

"I'll be damned," said Baily, "that's quite some story. I head El Tigre busted out of jail and no one knows where he is but you think he's come to Austin and snatched your wife?"

"I didn't say he did it. He ordered it done. He's very big on pay back and he thinks I've caused him to lose face by killing his assassin and helping to capture one. So, he's got this vendetta against me."

About that time the sound of a helicopter could be heard and a few minutes later in walked Tom Hatch, James White, several FBI agents, and technicians. White immediately called Baily aside and a somewhat heated discussion ensued. At its conclusion, Baily gathered his men, and they departed leaving the FBI in charge.

White joined Tom Hatch and Nate saying, "I hate to have do those things. I know the locals resent the hell out of us, but this really is a federal matter. By the way, Baily did tell me that the canvas of the neighbors only revealed one partial witness. Your next-door neighbor said he heard what sounded like a gunshot around 5:30 or 6:00. Curious, he looked out of his front window and saw two Mexicans carrying a big load of laundry out of your house and placing it in the rear of a blue unmarked van. After they subdued your wife, they must have wrapped her in a sheet to carry her outside. The guy did catch part of the license plate number. I'm going to add this information to the earlier A.P.B." he said while walking away.

"I came home later than usual today," said Nate. "I stopped to have a beer with one of the guys from the office whose wife had just delivered their first child. If I'd been here, they would have maybe shot me but maybe Jen would have been okay."

"Nate, you're not thinking straight."

"What do you mean?"

"I think this was always a snatch job. If the deal was to kill you, why bring the head? That would make no sense."

"No, I think this entire business was set up to make you suffer by worrying about Jen. El Tigre is known for his cruelty."

"Maybe you're right – but I got to get her back even if I play into his hands."

"Might not come to that," said White. We've got resources and assets that you have no inkling of. I'm putting them all in motion and all we can do right now is wait for one of those to come through. Right now, we don't have a clue as to where she might be."

“Well, I’m not waiting around, I’m heading to South Texas and when I find that little shit, I’m going to kill him!”

With that Nate walked into his bedroom and emerged a few minutes later with a small carry-on bag in one hand and his Army issue .45 and shoulder holster in the other.

“Hold on,” said White, “all you are going to do is get your butt in trouble. What we don’t need is a vigilante screwing around.”

“Ok, I’m going to be legal,” Nate assured him, grimly.

He turned and walked back into his bedroom where he placed a call to Sheriff Catalon in Eisenberg. After about fifteen minutes he re-entered the front room and went over to his fax machine. He retrieved several pages, signed one and faxed it and then walked back to Hatch and White and showed them the remaining page.

“I’m now an official reserve deputy sheriff of Bayon County, Texas, and in my official capacity, I can investigate the abduction of my wife and bring to justice the perpetrators.”

Tom Hatch said, “You’re serious so I’m coming with you – maybe I can keep you from being killed.”

White just threw up his hands and said, “Keep in touch.”

Chapter 21 – The Tiger Roams Free

"I told you to never contact me," said a deep Anglo voice.

"I know, I'm sorry but I'm in a bind. I need to pay my boys and I can't get my money. The feds are all over my ass."

"If you just tended to business instead of attracting attention to yourself, you'd be okay. What is that shit about? Cutting off heads and kidnapping women? You stupid dumbass. You got the feds buzzing around so none of us are safe. Oughta have your throat cut."

"That gringo son-of-a-bitch, he kill my boys. What am I supposed to do? Just let him ram it up my ass? I don't think so. I'm El Tigre, people treat me with respect."

"I understand that – all I'm saying is you should have squared things like we always do – on the q.t. *comprende*?"

"I can't change things now, can I? Maybe I could've handled it as you say, but I didn't. Now I gotta have seventy thousand or my boys will jump ship. You know their loyalty's pay day to pay day and I need them to get my network up and running again. I can pay you back easy then, it will be just like before."

"No, that's what I'm telling you. You really screwed up. It won't be business like before – at least for a good while. We have to be very very careful now, dot our i's and cross our t's like they say. I've never seen so many feds. They're swarming South Texas. They're rousting everyone – throwing a bunch of guys in jail for parole or probation violations – misdemeanor violations – everything they can think of. They're hoping someone with information will want to make a deal. We both know sooner or later someone will cop out, so we shut down until your screw up blows over. In the meantime, if you can't get across the river, and I can't help you, keep moving around unless you have a real secure place you can hole up in for several months." The Anglo voice continued, "I'll let you have the seventy grand but you'll owe me eighty in ninety days. Meet me at 2:00 a.m. day after tomorrow at the usual place and I'll bring you the money. I don't like it but I don't know who I can trust right now, so I'll bring it myself."

"Man, I don't know if I can pay you back that quickly. I mean you said we're shutting down, how am I gonna get the money?"

"Listen you fat bag of crap, don't give me that. You really don't want to piss me off more than you already have. I know you've got plenty of money stashed away. I'm giving you time to get to it. No damn excuses. One more thing, you better not screw up again." The line went dead.

El Tigre slowly hung up the phone in a phone booth on the outside of a convenience store in Del Rio. He was angry and sweating through his clothes. The night was warm, but his emotion caused most of the heat radiating from his body. It had been a long time since anyone had dared speak to him like that. Furthermore, the role of supplicant did not sit well. However, he knew this was his only chance – he had to have the money and he sure as hell couldn't go to a bank and take out a loan. As his breathing and heart rate returned to normal, he consoled himself with thoughts of payback.

Maybe one day, the big bosses across the river – the ones he never got to meet – would change their minds. They let him be the front man and appear to be the big man in South Texas, when, in fact, he worked under the gringo. He and his boys did all the work and took the risks while the arrogant white man sat back and issued orders. It wasn't fair and one day he'd do something about it. But not now. Now he had to recruit and rebuild his organization, deal with the money, and kill the man he knew would come after the woman. It was not a time to shut down. But he'd have to be very careful. He was as the saying went, between a rock and a hard place. The police and the Big Man.

Meanwhile, the Big Man, as he put down the phone, had thoughts of his own about the future. *I guess I'll have to take a drive over to Mexico and get permission to get rid of that fat ass. He's attracting way too much heat. If I do that and things calm down, wonder if the big bosses will let me out. I got millions in offshore accounts, me and Anita could go anywhere. We could live like royalty. Hell, more like a sultan – wonder how Anita would feel about a harem. He laughed out loud at the preposterous thought. Ain't gonna happen. But retirement did sound good. He was getting too old to deal with this kind of shit. Did he dare mention it? That itself was a risk. He'd have to think some more about the subject.*

Chapter 22 – La Leyenda

Nate and Hatch hitched a ride to San Antonio where Tom picked up his car. They drove to his house where Tom grabbed some clothes, kissed his wife and son, and hit the road south in the darkness.

"I hope we're not running ourselves out of the game by heading for the Rio Grande. I know you've got a hunch and your hunches have paid off in the past but man, if you're wrong, we are going to be way out of the action. Tell me why you think El Tigre is going to be found in South Texas. He could be anywhere."

"You're right," replied Nate. "It's just a hunch but the shortest way to Mexico is due south. I'm thinking the guys who snatched Jen will be trying to meet up with El Tigre as soon as possible and they'll all try to get across the river. I sure could be wrong, but I can't just do nothing while those people have my wife. Sure appreciate you throwing in with me."

"De nada."

They drove in silence, each man wrapped deeply in his thoughts. Suddenly the night was interrupted by the radio. The blue van had been discovered in the McCreless Mall shopping center parking lot in South San Antonio near the Highway 281 exit.

Nate asked, "Did they steal a car?"

"Nah," replied Tom. "They must have had someone waiting – at least no one at the center has a car missing that has been reported."

"Too bad," said Nate. "A description of a stolen car would have been helpful. Well, we at least know the direction to head."

The two men looked at each other for a long moment before Nate continued, "Sounds like a lead to me."

Tom grunted and pushed his foot down harder on the accelerator.

They arrived in Eisenberg as dawn broke. Too early to check in with the Sheriff, so they found a café that was open and ordered breakfast. They dawdled over their bacon and eggs, even ordered a third cup of coffee but it was still too early. However, Nate couldn't wait any longer and so they drove to the Sheriff's office and sat on a bench just inside the front door.

Their wait lasted almost an hour until Tony walked in. He was surprised to see them but invited them into his office. They declined his offer of coffee and took turns bringing him up to date on the kidnapping and the severed head of the gunman. Tony, of course, already knew of El Tigre's escape.

"I'm really sorry to hear about your wife, Nate. What can I do? My whole department will back your play."

"That's just it, Tony, I don't have a play. All we know or think we know is that the snatchers were headed south. Other than that, we don't have a clue. You got any snitches you could check with?"

"Nah, either the feds arrested them or scared them across the river. Let me think a minute." Tony leaned back in his chair and closed his eyes. There was no movement for so long Nate and Tom thought he'd fallen asleep. Suddenly Tony sat upright and snapped his fingers.

"There's a guy – a Mexican police captain across the river I worked with two or three years ago. He's honest and he knows the cartel inside out. He runs snitches and undercover cops over there. Far as I know, he's still alive even though he has a price on his head. He doesn't work out of the Reynosa

Police Department. He's some kind of a government guy. His name's Roberto Becerra. The only way to contact him is to go to Sadie's Double RR Saloon and talk to the owner, Jorge Escamilla. He speaks English. You can use my name and ask for a meet with Becerra. This Becerra guy he's *la leyenda* in Mexico. The story is the cartel killed his fiancé a week before their wedding. I guess the cartel thought they would make him back off with this warning. Didn't happen. It backfired on them. He hunts the cartels down without mercy. They say very few of the guys he arrests make it to trial. He's judge, jury and executioner and he's untouchable. He's rich, his family owns radio stations, newspapers, and a television station or two. He's well connected, they say he can call the president, day or night, and he'll respond. His grandfather was president of Mexico. His brother is a general in the Mexican Air Force and a cousin is minister of defense. No one gets elected in Mexico without his family's blessing and support."

"Wow! Pretty impressive," said Tom. "Thanks, Tony. You think this guy will work with us?"

"You're hunting the cartel, that's what he does full-time. Can't speak for him but I'd be surprised if he doesn't help you," said the Sheriff.

"Thanks again," said Tom. "You think this bar will be open this early?"

Tony laughed. "It never closes, it's a whorehouse in Boy's Town. I'll write down the address – probably better than asking around for it." With that he scribbled an address on a piece of paper and handed it to Tom.

Once back in their car, Nate said, "I know Tony said this place was open twenty-four-seven but somehow I think this guy moves around mostly at night."

"Makes sense in his business," said Tom. "I agree. I think we'd be wasting our time and maybe even sitting ourselves up if we went over there now. I think we wait until midnight or so."

"Sounds like a plan," said Nate.

So, they got motel rooms, napped, watched television, walked the floor, and did exercises until the time came to leave for Mexico.

Nate and Tom drove out onto the highway, down through McAllen and across the river to Reynosa. They were stopped by a Mexican border guard who asked about guns and drugs. They showed their identification cards and were told to dismount. They were shown into a small office where an overweight Mexican, referred to as "Captain," by their escort, in a wrinkled sweat-stained khaki uniform was sitting behind a battered desk.

He fingered the IDs but barely looked at them. "What do you want in Mexico?" he demanded. "Why are you armed? If this is official business, I should have been notified."

Nate replied, "We're not official, just drove over for a good steak and maybe a woman. The cartel knows us and we have to be able to defend ourselves."

"I see," replied the Mexican officer. "Bringing guns into Mexico for whatever reason is a serious matter. I think my duty demands that I fine you for this violation of our law."

"How much is the fine?" asked Hatch.

The Mexican looked up and down and stroked his chin while he calculated what these two gringos would pay without protest. Reaching a decision, he announced, "One thousand pesos each without a receipt. Two thousand with a receipt – administrative overhead. You understand?"

“We understand,” said Nate and Tom, almost in unison, while reaching for their wallets.

They were allowed back to their car and soon were off on the main highway looking for their exit. It came up shortly and the street they turned on ran out of pavement and streetlights after three blocks. They had only their headlights to guide them toward a glow in the night sky. The road was narrow and pockmarked. There was only an occasional light that emanated from the dark hulks of buildings on either side of them, whether homes or businesses, they couldn’t tell. The road became worse, and the car rocked from side to side as it drove into one hole and then another. However, with each agonizing bounce and twist, the glow ahead became nearer until all at once they hit pavement and what passed for civilization in Boys’ Town.

There the streets were paved for a number of blocks. Streetlights blazed, neon signs dazzled the eye, cars and pickup trucks with American license plates lined each side of the street. Every two or three had a Mexican guardian sitting on its hood or leaning against it. The street and sidewalks were filled with American teenagers and college age boys, most of them drunk or near drunk, yelling to each other, laughing, singing, staggering, some falling down, all making noise. The din was all the louder for the silent streets Tom and Nate had just passed through.

Hatch observed out loud, “This must be the Mexican version of Dante’s Inferno. “

“Just a bunch of guys doing the Texan coming of age,” replied Nate.

Bars with their neon lit exteriors lined each side of the street, interrupted occasionally by a café or souvenir shop or liquor store. Grass grew in cracks of the sidewalks and pavement. Trash and litter rested beneath each parked car and in between buildings. A lazy breeze sporadically blew bits of paper down the street. They found a place in someone's yard to park on a side street and paid the homeowner handsomely to watch their vehicle. They then walked into the inferno as Hatch had described the scene they entered. After walking a block and a half they found Sadie's Double RR Saloon.

It was much larger inside than it appeared from the outside. The din inside was louder than outside. There was a juke box just inside and to the right of the door playing some Mexican music that no one was paying attention to. The long bar was to the left decorated with American young men holding on with one hand with a drink or a whore in the other. The center of the room was filled with mismatched tables and chairs. Most were filled with American youths, some with women on their laps, some chairs holding a woman. All the tabletops were filled with beer bottles, some partially full, most empty, leaving wet circles on the tabletops. Ash trays were filled to overflowing. Cigarette smoke formed a feathery blue haze that floated slightly above head high. The place smelled of stale beer, cigarettes, cheap perfume, perspiration and sex. Loud drunken male voices competed with alternating choruses of the "Eyes of Texas" and the "Aggie War Hymn", the music from the jukebox, and the click clack of glasses and bottles. The din was nearly ear splitting. Out on the small dance floor half a dozen or so couples were making a show of dancing while barely managing to stay upright. The forced shrill laughter of women did not reach their eyes which were unfocused, dull and tired. Hatch surveyed the room. There were no more than ten people in the crowd over the age of thirty. He and Nate made their way to the bar and ordered two Carta Blancas. They asked the large dark bartender if the owner was around and if he was, could they speak to him?

There was no reply so they found an empty table and sat down intending to ask a waitress the same questions when one went by. There they sat sipping their beers and nervously peeling the labels when unannounced a Mexican of average size wearing dark trousers, a white shirt, and a bolo tie sat down at their table.

"I am Jorge Escamilla, the owner, what can I do for you?"

"We're American police officers and we came across to speak with Captain Becerra about a matter of mutual interest. Sheriff Tony Catalon over in Eisenberg said his name was familiar to Becerra and would get us an introduction. Is that right?" asked Hatch.

Escamilla did not reply, instead he just stared at the two of them. Finally, as the silence became uncomfortable, Nate said,

"Look we're not here to play games. El Tigre has kidnapped my wife and we want to find him and get her back. Either you will help us or not but I'm tired of the fisheyes!"

Ignoring this outburst, Jorge signaled a waitress who handed him two menus. He handed one each to Tom and Nate and said,

"Unobtrusively as you can, slip your credential inside these and slide them back." He gathered the menus and rose from his seat. "I will check these out and return. Meanwhile, I have a small kitchen. The steak and eggs are good if you are hungry."

With that he disappeared into the crowd. A waitress, undoubtedly under orders, came up to their table. They hadn't eaten since lunch, so they followed Jorge's recommendation and ordered steaks, eggs, and another beer and settled down to wait for whatever came next. Two hours passed and they were both getting antsy when Jorge reappeared.

"Wait five minutes and make your way to the men's room – marked "hombres' – if you don't know Spanish. When you are sure you are alone, turn the middle coat hook above the mirror three hundred and sixty degrees. Roberto is waiting behind the mirror." With that he returned their credentials, rose from his chair and was gone in the crowded dance floor.

Tom and Nate waited, as instructed, and then made their way around behind the bar to the men's restroom. There was no one there. The space was small and presented the usual accommodations. The only thing unusual was the full length mirror.

"Well, here we go," said Hatch. "Think we can trust this guy? He sounds like a guy who shoots first and then talks. All this secret door and stuff makes me a little nervous. What about you?"

"It's all a little strange, I agree," said Nate. "But here we are, we're in their parlor, so to speak, what choice do we have, except to go along with their play, keep our eyes open, hope for the best and keep our weapons handy."

"Guess that's about it," Tom Hatch took a deep breath. "Too late to turn back."

Tom kept watch by the door while Nate turned the middle coat hook. Silently the mirror opened as a doorway revealing nothing but darkness. Quickly Tom and Nate slipped through the opening and pulled the door shut behind them. They stood in darkness for several minutes then all of a sudden, a spotlight bathed them in its brilliant light. They were momentarily blinded. Then as quickly as the spot had come on, it went off to be replaced by several low lights in the ceiling.

The room they were in was no more than eight feet wide and fifteen or sixteen feet long. The floor was concrete but was covered with several thick rugs. The walls were bare. At the far end of the room was a desk with an AK-47 lying on it. File cabinets covered the near wall. To the right side of the desk there was a door obviously leading to the outside.

Behind the desk stood a man slightly over six feet with the build of an athlete. His hair was black and curly and fell almost to his shoulders. He affected a goatee and a thin mustache below his nose. He was dressed in slim jeans, scuffed cowboy boots, and a white tee shirt with a pack of cigarettes rolled up in his left sleeve. His eyes were dark and as he gazed at the two men, his eyes took on the intensity of black opals.

"I am Roberto Becerra," he announced in a voice with no accent, "what can I do for you?"

Tom Hatch spoke up. "We want to find El Tigre." He went on to explain not only the kidnapping but the jail escape as well.

"I'm really sorry to hear about your wife," Roberto said to Nate. "El Tigre is a mean little shit. But since he doesn't operate on this side of the river, I haven't been keeping tabs on him. However, some of my snitches may know something. I don't know how they do it, but information flows through these gangs faster than the T.V. news. I might find someone who will talk. El Tigre is not well respected. Don't get me wrong, he's dangerous and people still fear him but the word on the street is he isn't even in charge of South Texas, like he claims to be. The real boss in South Texas is an Anglo. No one seems to know who he is. He's the one who set up the distribution system, sets the price, protects the territory and the like. El Tigre supplies the muscle and recruits the enforcers as well as the mules. As far as organization on the scale of the cartels, forget it. El Tigre couldn't organize a three-car funeral."

"That may all be true," said Nate, "but he's got my wife and I want him."

"I understand – believe me. I'll help you all I can, but it may take some time. In the meanwhile, you two need to stay out of sight. You may as well be carrying signs saying, 'I'm a cop.' Jorge will take care of you. He has some very nice rooms for special guests. You can trust him because I trust him. He is married to my second cousin. If I come up with anything, Jorge will let you know. I understand this is urgent and I will move as fast as I can. Now go back the way you came. The mirror is two-way so you can check the room first. The release is a button on the right side of the mirror. Find Jorge and tell him you need the special rooms."

Nate and Tom exited the men's room without incident and found Jorge behind the bar.

He listened as they made their request then said, "Wait a couple of minutes after I leave then casually walk to the kitchen."

They did as were instructed and found Jorge in the middle of the bedlam that was the kitchen. Cooks and waitpersons were flying around. There were orders shouted either to fill or pick up. It was hot but filled with delicious aromas. Before they could investigate the sources of these smells, Jorge was urging them to a closet. As they entered, they were confronted with shelves of canned goods, bags of various ingredients and boxes of others. When they were inside and the door closed, Jorge tugged at a certain shelf. It rolled away to reveal a stairway.

"Man, you guys are like James Bond or something," observed Hatch.

Jorge made no reply but began climbing a metal spiral stairway. Once they were on the floor above, Jorge motioned to follow him along the corridor. Within a few steps they came to a door. When opened, a modern hotel room was revealed, together with a bath. He walked over and unlocked a connecting door that revealed a duplicate room.

"I'll have snacks and beer brought up. If you need anything, there are telephones in each room that connect only to my office, all you have to do is call me," said Jorge. With that he left. Hatch and Tom took off their coats and ties and proceeded to make themselves at home.

"Wish we could contact my office," said Hatch. "Hate to be isolated like this."

"Know what you mean," said Nate. "I probably hate it worse than you but these guys are doing us a favor at the risk of their lives, so I have to respect that."

Their isolation, except for the young lady who brought their food and beer, lasted eighteen hours. Finally, Jorge came for them. Once more they made their way to the men's room and through the mirror and once again found Roberto seated behind his desk.

Chapter 23 – On the Trail of the Tiger

Roberto now wore a black shirt and a black duster beneath which hung his AK-47.

"I have made contact with one of my snitches. He has agreed to meet us and by the way, he says he may have some information to help us. I've used this hombre several times and his intel has been good, but you can't trust any of these people. So, we go armed. What are you carrying?" Hatch and Nate showed their weapons, Nate's passed Roberto's scrutiny but not Tom's. "A six-shot revolver? You may as well throw rocks. Here, take this," whereupon Roberto handed him a Glock 18 and three full magazines. "If you don't know this weapon, each mag has nineteen rounds and can be fired full auto, just turn the selector switch counterclockwise down."

"You think we'll need all this fire power?" said Nate. "I thought this was a good guy."

"Friend, there are no good guys where we are going. Trust no one and hope for the best."

With that familiar homily ringing in their ears, Tom and Nate joined Roberto and slipped out of the side door and into a small shed used to house the electric, water and gas meters and then into an alleyway. They turned left and, in the darkness, walked half a city block to a street where an aging Ford sedan was parked. As they seated themselves with Roberto behind the wheel, he said, "don't be put off by appearances, this baby is partially armored and has a new 375 horsepower motor. It can outrun anything in town." With that he turned on the engine and they were off. After several blocks, Roberto turned on the headlights as they drove through dark pock-marked streets. Now and then, they would come to a street with streetlights and some traffic but on the whole of their journey, they met relatively few cars, no police and no pedestrians. Except for Boys Town, the city slept. After forty minutes, Roberto pulled to the curb and stopped the car.

"This guy has a room in that old apartment building in the middle of the next block. I've been here before. There's no elevator so we'll have to climb the stairs to the third floor. We'll be exposed for the full time we are on the stairs, so watch for an ambush, these guys work for whoever pays them last. Ready?"

"Let's do it," replied Nate. They exited the car and walked close to the building wall, hurried across the street, and stopped at the front door of the apartment building. It was unlocked and all three quickly moved inside. The stairway was just ahead, with a dirty carpet runner leading upstairs to the dimly lit landing to the upper floors.

Roberto took the lead, his AK-47 now pointing the way. Hatch followed four or five paces back and next to the stair railing. Nate followed by the same distance but near the opposite side of the stairway. They reached the second-floor landing where the corridor extended to their left and right. Roberto had made the turn and was up several stair steps leading to the third floor when automatic fire belched out from above. Roberto and Tom threw themselves down while Nate edged around the corner of the hallway to his right. As he did so, he noticed the door just ahead of him move. He grabbed the doorknob and quickly flung the door open. The Mexican gunman hiding there was thrown off balance and staggered out into the hallway. Nate hit him a vicious blow with the barrel of his .45 and the man dropped to the floor unmoving. Nate picked up his AK-47 and bent over him and quickly used the man's belt and his own to secure the gunman's arms and legs.

All at once there came a burst of automatic weapons fire from downstairs. Since none of the three of them were visible from the first floor, Nate figured it had to be covering fire. Sure enough, as he peeped around the corner, there was a gunman creeping up the stairs. Nate pointed the confiscated AK-47 around the corner and sprayed the stairwell on full auto. Almost immediately came the shout of *merida* and the sound of feet storming down the stairs. Nate chanced another peep and saw an AK-47 discorded on the stairs and a slight figure running out the front door. *Guess he hadn't bargained on anyone shooting back*, thought Nate.

"Two down," Nate shouted to Roberto and Hatch. "I'll finish it then," said Roberto as he rose up on one knee and riddled the third-floor door. Then silence. Roberto crept up the stairs and along the wall and, as Tom arrived by his side, he kicked the center panel of the thin door. It shattered. Behind it lay the body of one of the would-be assailants.

Roberto and Hatch moved into the room and saw another figure lying near the windows in a pool of blood. Roberto turned the body over. "That's my snitch," he said.

"How did they know we were coming?" wondered Tom out loud. "Only the three of us and the snitch knew we were coming to talk to him."

"My guess," said Roberto, "he wanted to score points and told the cartel guys about the meet. They set up the ambush and killed him because he had talked to me. They couldn't trust him anymore. Nate is your guy alive?"

"Don't know – hit him pretty hard" said Nate as he joined the others.

"Let's go see if he's alive, maybe I can get something out of him," said Roberto. They retreated to the second floor and found the gunman awake and struggling against his bonds. "Grab ahold, let's take him upstairs where we can have a private conversation," ordered Roberto.

The would-be assassin was manhandled up the stairs and bound in a chair in the snitch's room with a length of nylon cord produced by Roberto.

"You speak English?" asked Roberto.

"*Un poco*," said the frightened gunman.

"Well, you better understand this," said Roberto. "If you want to leave here alive, you'll tell us what we want to know. Where is the woman, the senora? Where is El Tigre?"

"*Ni* idea."

"I'll *ni* idea you," said Roberto, as he jammed the barrel of his AK-47 into the ear of the bound man. He would have fallen on his back in reaction to the sudden pain were it not for Hatch's quick action in grabbing him by his shoulders.

Upon being restored to an upright position, the captive, with a look of horror on his face, blurted out, "*Por favor*," followed by a rapid burst of Spanish which Tom and Nate, in their limited grasp of the language, took to mean he was pleading not to be killed. As for the rest of it, Tom, with a slightly better understanding of Spanish, since as a Mormon, he had served his mission in Puerto Rico, turned to Nate.

"He's saying he was paid two hundred American to come to this place and shoot some gringos. Also, the man Roberto shot on the third floor, he says killed the man by the window. He doesn't know why. Says he never heard of a woman or El Tigre."

"You lying piece of shit," shouted Nate, pushing Roberto aside and bringing up his .45 to within inches of the Mexican's face. “Answer the questions or I’m going to blow a hole in your damn head.”

“Senor, por favor,” he pleaded, “I cannot tell you what I do not know. *Por favor no hagas esto.”*

“I warned you,” said Nate. He began a slow squeeze of the trigger and at the last millisecond moved his pistol so that when it fired, the round only took off the tip of the bound man’s ear. The prisoner screamed in pain and wet himself. The noise of the gunshot in the small room temporarily deafened everyone. Through the haze of the smoke and the smell of cordite, Hatch was the first to recover.

“Geeze Nate,” he said. “We’re law enforcement, you can’t do that to a prisoner.”

“I told you, I’ll do whatever it takes to get Jen back.” With that Nate turned back to the bound man and slapped him several times until he stopped screaming and Nate had his full attention. “Now you know I’m not fooling around, tell me who hired you. Are you a member of the cartel?”

The prisoner’s ear was bleeding down the side of his face and coloring his dingy shirt a dark red. His eyes were nearly popping out of his head, and he was struggling to breathe. Slowly and with great effort, he spoke haltingly in Spanish. Roberto turned to Nate and Tom and translated.

“He says to please help him, his ear hurts so much. He knows nothing of the cartel or a woman. He’s heard of El Tigre but doesn’t work for him. He says he has no job, and he does whatever he can to make some money. He is not a bad man. A man he knows as Miguel Chaves hires him now and then for odd jobs. He’s the one that gave him the money and gun. It was the first time he had ever been hired to shoot someone. That’s all he knows.” Roberto, then asked him in

Spanish where he could find this Miguel Chaves and what did he look like? After several painful minutes, their prisoner replied haltingly in Spanish.

Again, Roberto translated. "He says he meets this guy at the *Mercado de Agrieuetos*. He's there most days and he always has money and jobs. Says he's big man, bigger than me. He has a shaved head and a pockmarked face. He has a reputation for being a very mean man." Roberto added, "Sounds like some kind of a recruiter or headhunter to me." Then Roberto turned back to the man in the chair and asked him in Spanish if there was anything else he could tell them.

The man shook his head and said, "*Por favor*, help me. Let me go. *No se lo digo a nadie. Por favor*, I tell no one."

"Sure, okay let's go," said Roberto. He hung back as Nate and Tom left the room. There was the sound of a small caliber pistol and when they rushed back into the room, the Mexican had acquired a third eye. Roberto was stuffing a small automatic back into his boot.

He shrugged, "This is worse than a war over here. There are no rules or treaties. He would have contacted this Miguel as soon as he got free and told him we would be looking for him. I didn't want to walk into another ambush. Now, you two can come with me or you can go back across the river, and I'll go back to my snitches. Your call."

Hatch and Nate could barely tear their eyes away from the inert body in the chair, much less speak. Finally, as he accumulated enough saliva to speak, Nate said, "I'm in." He and Roberto turned to look at Tom whose face had lost all coloring. After several long minutes, Tom slowly nodded.

They trooped down the stairs and back to Roberto's car. All this time, not a light had come on in any of the apartments, not a head had peeked out of a doorway, not a siren was heard heralding the arrival of the police.

Tom Hatch remarked upon this strange phenomenon. As he pulled the car away from the curb, Roberto shrugged and replied,

"I told you over here, it is worse than a war."

When Nate and Tom reached their rooms at the Double RR, they were too keyed up to sleep. They had room service deliver a six pack. After they had each drank two apiece, Nate said, "You want to talk 'bout it?"

"What I want to do is forget it, but I know I never will," replied Hatch. "Even in this place I can't believe an officer of the law would cold bloodedly kill a bound prisoner and, while I'm at it, I might as well tell you I was surprised and shocked by you. I know you feel justified because of your wife but torture of a prisoner is way over the line."

"Tom, I know you're right and I can't explain nor justify my actions. I can only hope you'll hang with me. Jen and I need your help."

Hatch arose from his chair and looked at Nate for a long time. He shook his head and in a low sad voice said, "Our humanity is the only thing that separates us from these people and it's not a thing you can turn off and on." With that he walked into his room and shut the door.

Chapter 24 – Shaven Head

Hatch finally joined Nate and Roberto the next morning in the alley behind Sofie's. Roberto was driving a light blue van and explained that if they spotted Chaves anywhere near a street, he intended to grab him and throw him into the van and then drive to a safe house. If they couldn't grab him, they'd have to take him wherever they found him and improvise the interrogation. Hatch and Nate both took a seat in the van.

Once again, they were driving down alleyways but stopping at each intersection to avoid the oncoming vehicles. Mexican drivers, it seemed were unaware of brakes and relied on their horns instead. Also, it appeared that they believed the faster they went, the safer they were. It therefore was a time-consuming proposition to move across town but after close to an hour they reached their destination – the market.

The market occupied the better part of a city block on the eastern edge of the commercial district. As they exited the van, Roberto handed each of them a small radio.

"We'll have to split up and look for the guy. If you spot him, let the other two know where you are and where he is. We'll meet and decide what to do. Any questions? Okay, good hunting."

The market had just opened and many vendors were still setting out their wares. Others, offering fruit or vegetables were washing them down. The food vendors were hard at work and the smells announced their presence. Pleasant smells of heated cooking oil or wood fires, the sizzle of onions and garlic, the pat pat of the women making tortillas, all threatened to overcome the senses. Especially those who had not eaten since the previous evening. Before them spread an almost unbelievable array of sights, sounds and smells. Merchants calling out their products, the rainbow of colors presented by the fresh fruits and vegetables – greens, reds, yellow and even purple. The intoxicating smells wafting from the small stoves of the food stalls-quesadillas, tacos and gorditas. The colorful costumes of the bustling, cheerful shoppers. The Tex-Mex culture of Austin had not prepared Nate for this. Nate's stomach began to growl but he fought against the temptation and continued to push his way through the gathering crowd which consisted mostly of women with a basket on their arm, a baby on their shoulder or a toddler by the hand. The vendors were hawking their offerings and the customers were checking them out or bargaining about the price. The noise was considerable and seemed to rise and fall for no apparent reason.

Soon the three reached the central plaza which consisted of a small area of dead grass and a fountain covered in algae where water slowly seeped down the sides of the concrete angel in its center. This was apparently the area where day workers gathered each morning to wait to be hired. There were several men standing around the fountain offering to hire workers for various types of work. Either the work or the pay was not to their liking, who is to say, for there were few takers for whatever was being offered. The crowd seemed determined to wait in hopes of better offers. There was no sign of anyone matching the description of Miguel. The three split up and took positions at different locations around the plaza.

The sun, by now, had fully risen and as the temperature began to rise, so too did the temperament of those waiting. Several voices now began berating the men at the fountain, apparently due to their meager offerings. Heads were nodding and now mutterings could be heard from various sources in the assembly. This all changed in an instant as a tall man with a shaven head and a pocked-marked face strode through the gathering and headed for the fountain. An undertone of anticipation seemed now to flow through the group as Shaven Head turned to face them. The crowd, composed almost entirely of men, most standing, a few sitting on the ground and some sitting on the few benches scattered about, seemed willing to stay its agitation so long as his announcements were palatable, but no longer.

Shaven Head began reading from a paper in his hand, pausing after each job and pay was read off to allow those interested to raise their hands. These were then directed to various locations to be driven to the job sites by the waiting pickup trucks. The three had now rejoined each other and Roberto translated as Shaven Head read off the last item on his list. Two men with knowledge of firearms were needed for three days. At least one must be able to operate an automobile. The jobs paid one hundred American per day.

There was no immediate response from the gathered men, each no doubt mulling over in his mind the unspoken fact that these jobs involved not only illegal activity but danger as well. Finally, two young men held up their hands. They were told to accompany the one with the shaven head.

Roberto turned to his companions, commenting, “Where else would you find gangsters being recruited the same as day laborers? We need to get back to the van so we can follow this guy.”

“You two go get the van, one of us needs to follow on foot,” said Tom Hatch.

“Makes sense,” said Roberto as he turned to leave.

Hatch watched as the person they all believed to be Miguel, finished his business. He signaled to the two waiting men who followed him out of the market onto an adjoining city street. Hatch followed taking care not to be conspicuous. After walking two blocks, the trio turned into the front door of a three-story brick building which, like the others on the street, had its entrance area covered by graffiti. Hatch hung back a few minutes then entered the lobby which, as he'd hoped, contained a list of the building tenants in a glass enclosed display. It seemed to contain professionals, doctors, lawyers, dentists, insurance agencies and finally, Chaves Impresas at room 306. Hatch went out on the street and stopped two doors down and leaned against the wall. When the van appeared Hatch quickly jumped in and told Roberto to keep going. As they drove for several blocks, he told the others about Miguel's office. They pulled into a nearby side street.

After considering their options, they decided to park where they could observe the building. If Chaves came out, they would grab him and throw him into the van and take him to one of Roberto's safehouses to interrogate him. If he didn't come out by the time the other tenants closed up, they would storm his office and question him there. So, they found a good observation place and waited.

The building where Chaves officed was on a fairly busy street. All day long cars, trucks, buses, tractors, even horse-drawn farm wagons moved up and down in front of them. As there were no bars or restaurants nearby, there were few pedestrians on the sidewalk so that their surveillance was unrewarded.

Around six-thirty the building began to disgorge its inhabitants, but no sign of Chaves. After waiting until the flow of occupants had stopped, Nate said,

"I guess we go in after him. Any ideas on how we handle this?"

Hatch spoke up, "I know we saw the two new recruits leave, but we have no idea who, besides Chaves might be in the office with him."

"I know," said Nate, "but I'm not waiting. I think the three of us ought to be able to handle however many there are. After all, he can't have an army in there."

"I think there will be no one but him in there," said Roberto. "He's no threat to the gangs, he works for all of them I bet, so he won't need bodyguards. Since he's in the shady stuff, he won't trust a secretary, so I say we just go get him."

"Okay, that makes sense," said Hatch. "I'm ready."

"Me too," said Nate.

They entered the building and made their way up to the offices of Chaves Enterprises. Roberto tried the door. It was locked. He knocked on the door.

"Who's there?" came a voice from inside.

"You don't know me," answered Roberto, "But I have a message from a mutual friend."

"Pass it under the door."

"I can't do that, its oral and I'm not gonna take the chance of being overheard out here in the corridor. If you don't want to let me in to deliver the message, that's okay with me. I'll just go back and tell our friends you've decided you no longer want to work with them. I don't think I need remind you what that will mean. *Adios*."

"No, wait!" and the door rattled as a key was inserted in the lock and turned. The door opened and Roberto entered.

Shaven Head snarled, "Okay. You're in, what's the message?"

"This," said Roberto as he brought up his pistol which he's been holding behind his hip. At this moment Nate and Tom entered the small office with guns drawn.

"What the shit is this?" asked Chaves. "I don't have any money here. I have connections who will not be happy if harm comes to me. What do you want?"

"We're not worried about your connections," said Roberto. "They don't know us. As to harm coming to you that's totally up to you, tell us what we want to know and we'll leave and you'll be fine."

"This is bullshit, I don't know what you want to know, but I tell you straight whether I know the answer or not, I'm not talking to you."

With this, Roberto swung his pistol and struck Chaves just above his left eye. Blood spurted out and Chaves staggered back and was prevented from falling only because he staggered back against his desk. Momentarily, his eyes glazed over. He shook his head and made as though he was going to launch himself at Roberto but Roberto dissuaded him of that intention by placing his automatic against the forehead of Chaves.

"Make one move and you're a dead man," Roberto commanded. "Sit down in that chair, put your arms in back." As he complied, Tom swiftly tied Chaves' arms and legs.

"Now what?" asked Chaves.

"I'm glad you're speaking English," said Hatch. "That'll help avoid misunderstandings."

"I don't have no misunderstandings," said Chaves. "You're all dead men." By now blood had run down his face onto his shirt collar and his left eye was almost swollen closed so that the attempted bravado was almost ludicrous. No one laughed.

Instead, Hatch demanded, "Knock off the silly tough guy stuff. It's not working and frankly, coming from someone in your predicament, it's downright stupid. Now you appear to be an ambitious and reasonably intelligent person so I'm going to talk to you the same way. Keep quiet and listen. We need you to tell us the whereabouts of El Tigre and the location of where he's holding the lady he kidnapped."

"I don't know nothing about a tiger or a woman!"

"Mr. Chaves you are on the verge of disappointing me – I thought you were smarter than that. But okay, I'll spell it out; I don't know why you work for the cartel, really makes no difference in the long run. Whether its loyalty or fear, if you cross them, you know they will not only kill you but everyone in your family. You also know they don't spend any time investigating rumors of disloyalty. A hint and they act and then just recruit someone new. So, here's the deal, either you tell us what we need to know, or we'll spread the word on the street that we turned you and now you're an informer. What's your life expectancy then? For sure, no one's going to sell you any life insurance, are they?"

Chaves now seemed to be having trouble focusing his eyes. He kept licking his lips and twisting his head as though expecting help to arrive. Finally, he gave a deep sigh as his body seemed to shrink in on itself and in a quiet still voice asked,

"How do I know I can trust you?"

"You hear what I just said?" asked Tom. "You don't have any choice, so quit stalling, we're running out of time here."

"Look, I only met this El Tigre once. He invited some of us contractors to a big party up in Juarez. He's got a big ranch just northwest of town. I have no idea where he is and I swear I don't know nothing about no woman. The only other thing I can tell you is he owns a nightclub in Juarez and has an apartment above it. Rumor is he entertains women there. The club is called "Honest Abe's."

"Of course, it is," said Hatch.

"That's all I can tell you," Chaves replied. "Now will you let me go?"

"Come on guys," said Nate, "leave him, he'll eventually get loose, or someone will find him. As for you," he said, pointing his .45 at Chaves, "If you tell anyone about us, what we said still goes."

Chapter 25 – Tracking the Tiger

They made their way out of the building and back to Roberto's van. They then set out for the sixteen-kilometer drive to General Lucio Blanco International Airport. About five kilometers short of the airport, traffic was blocked by two black pickup trucks pulled across the highway.

"Marine check point," said Roberto. "Sit tight, don't make a sudden move. These guys are even more trigger happy than the gangsters. So just let me handle things."

Up ahead heavily armed men, all in black, with balaclavas covering their heads swarmed the slow-moving column of vehicles. Finally, when theirs was the front most automobile, Roberto held his credentials out the window and spoke rapidly in Spanish to the nearest Marine. Roberto was directed to drive off the roadway and to then dismount and accompany the young Marine to an apparent superior. The two of them spoke, Roberto again showed his papers, there was much pointing by both men in the direction of Nate and Tom. Finally, the officer spoke on a radio mounted in one of the pickups. Again, there were many gestures, nods of the head and finally the officer handed Roberto's credentials back to him with a dismissive jerk of his hand.

Roberto returned to the van, started it and drove off without a word. After being sure that they were clear of the roadblock, Roberto explained, "These guys recognize no authority except their immediate commander. I thought I'd never get the arrogant little son-of-a-bitch to call my boss. Anyway, he finally did and we're clear for the airport."

At the airport, they were fortunate to be able to book a flight to Juarez leaving in an hour and a half. They got some food and drank a couple of beers and then boarded the aircraft for the four-hour flight to Abraham Gonzalez International Airport. The flight was uneventful, and they arrived on time. They made their way to the car rental counter and rented a car and got instructions and a map to the location of Honest Abe's in downtown Juarez. They found it on the Boulevard M Gomez Morin. Even at this late hour it was a busy and animated venue.

As their eyes and ears adjusted to the scene before them, they could see the interior of the club was divided into two sections. The one to their left contained a restaurant with tables covered with white cloths with a band playing dance music. The area was populated by well-dressed couples. Around a corner and set far back was a long bar with pole dancers and strippers. Piped in music pumped out indescribable sounds, almost primeval in its intensity. In the center of the floor, two naked well-toned women wrestled in the mud. This area was populated completely by men.

"Something for everyone, it looks like," Nate commented. "What do we do now?"

Roberto answered, "I suggest we get a table and check things out."

They were no sooner seated than three scantily clad women descended upon them. Hatch came out of his chair like he'd been hit with a cattle prod when one of the ladies stuck her tongue in his ear and asked him to buy her a bottle of champagne. The other two women forced their way onto the laps of Roberto and Nate offering private lap dances and asking for champagne. Roberto unleashed a torrent of Spanish, and the women made their exits as quickly as they'd made their entrances.

"What'd you say to them?" Nate wondered.

Roberto replied, "I told them we were all gay and were waiting for our lovers."

A waitress took their orders for three Carta Blancas and was back in minutes with three ice-cold bottles.

"What you told those three gals sure worked," said Hatch. "But you're not, I mean, if you are, it's okay," he stammered turning red. "I mean . . . "

"Not to worry Tom," Roberto was laughing, "you're safe with me."

"Really, I'm sorry about that," said Tom, "it just slipped out."

"I understand, forget it," said Roberto. "Do either of you see an entrance to the apartment upstairs?" Nate and Tom shook their heads. "I assume there'd be a guard or two at the entrance," Roberto explained, "and I see no sign of that. The restrooms are behind the bar and there's a lot of coming and going so I imagine a guarded door would raise questions so I doubt it would be back there. The trouble is there's no other place for it to be."

"Gotta be outside then," Nate agreed. "Let's drink up, pay our bill, and recon outside."

"Sounds right to me," Tom set down his empty beer bottle and threw a handful of pesos on the table. "Let's go have a look."

They pushed their way through the crowd at the door and made their way to the sidewalk. The difference in temperature from the super cool club to the sticky outside almost took their breaths away. This coupled with the noise of the traffic and the flashing neon lights momentarily left them confused. However, they quickly gathered their wits and began walking to their left as that was the nearest intersection. They turned left again when they reached the intersection and continued parallel with the side street until they reached a narrow dark passageway. It was lined with overflowing dumpsters, newspapers, broken bottles, a condom or two, fast food wrappers, and all of the other detritus of modern civilization. The three proceeded cautiously, practically feeling their way. All of the buildings they passed had exits to this alleyway but, at least in the case of the club, the narrow doorway they reckoned to give access to it, proved only to lead to the kitchen.

They stood in the shadows for over two hours and all that came in or went out the door was obviously kitchen employees. Some spent a few minutes outside to smoke a cigarette, some came out to dump garbage in the already overflowing dumpster, and others in and out on less obvious errands.

Finally, they agreed that it was unlikely that the alleyway door led to the upstairs. The alley itself was too narrow, what with the dumpsters scattered along it, for the easy passage of a car. They couldn't see El Tigre coming and going through the evil smelling trash littered passage. The entrance to the upstairs had to be inside the club so they retraced their steps and reclaimed their table. No sooner were they seated than their table was approached by three large Mexicans. The one in the lead, who appeared to be in charge, spoke English as he reached their table,

"Well, well, the three queers are back. I don't think we need your kind in here. I invite you to leave or we'll carry you out."

With one swift motion, Roberto had withdrawn his small pistol and rammed it into the crotch of the speaker whose eyes bulged out as he doubled over in pain. "Tell your compadres to back off or I'll make a eunuch out of you. Nod if you understand." The man quickly nodded and uttered instructions in Spanish to his companions who retreated to the rear of the club.

"All right now, get a smile on your ugly face and lead us to the entrance of the upstairs." The man started to protest but was cut short by a jab of the automatic in Roberto's hand. They stood and Roberto placed his pistol inside the Mexican's coat and with an occasional jab in the ribs he led them into the adjoining room, winding in and out between the tables and the seated patrons. They paused at a small alcove where the restrooms were located. There was an unmarked double door. Following a vicious jab in his ribs, the Mexican moved aside a painting and pressed a button. The doors swung open revealing an elevator. With another prod from Roberto, the Mexican entered the elevator, closely followed by Roberto, Tom and Nate.

Soon, the door slid open and they found themselves in a small vestibule facing a startled Mexican seated in a chair beside an ornate doorway. Roberto pointed his pistol and motioned for him to raise his hands and stand up. The guard did as was instructed and Nate quickly relieved him of his sidearm. Roberto motioned to the two Mexicans to be quiet as he tried the door. It was unlocked. Hatch had the Mexicans lay down with their arms crossed on top of their heads.

Roberto nodded and slowly opened the door. He and Nate moved into the entryway with guns held in front in the shooter's position. Moving their heads from side to side, they slowly advanced into the large living room. Facing them was a wall of windows. In the center of the room, suited out with expensive Mexican modern furniture, a twenty something very pretty female sat on a dark leather couch with one leg propped up on the coffee table in front of her. She was busy applying bright red nail polish to her toes. She was dressed only in panties and a bra and had not noticed the silent approach of Nate and Roberto.

For some reason she turned her head and saw them. The bottle of nail polish flew up in the air as she screamed and bolted from the room.

Roberto ran after her and Nate moved into the adjoining dining room and kitchen. A silly thought entered his mind. *No way was that nail polish going to come out of the carpet. Buy a new carpet or move the couch over a few inches to cover the stain? What would El Tigre do?*

The dining room was large and contained a table and chairs that would accommodate sixteen people. Over the center of the table hung a massive crystal chandelier. Large mirrors along the walls reflected the light and projected a soft glow to several oil paintings on the far wall. Not high art, but Nate thought they were well done, he didn't recognize the artists.

Nate entered the white very modern kitchen. He found himself admiring the taste of whoever had decorated the apartment. On the center counter lay what appeared to be a dozen each of orange and red roses, along with some velvety frosted sage. There were green leaves lying next to several empty crystal vases. A crystal bowl of bright red berries sat nearby. Nate assumed the young lady had decided to do her toes before arranging the roses.

As he re-entered the living room, he saw Roberto had managed to grab the young lady before she could get down the hallway. She was cussing, crying, and screaming all at once while she was struggling to free herself from Roberto's grasp.

For his part, Roberto was trying to hold just her arms but with her twisting around his hands slid to other parts of her body. He was clearly embarrassed and looked to Nate for help. Nate grinned and shrugged his shoulders as he moved down the hallway.

The first door he came to was open: a small powder room. The next doorway also had an open door. He shoved his weapon inside and followed it. The room was an empty bedroom and bath. The last door led to a huge master bedroom, also empty. Nate holstered his gun and began searching the room. He couldn't help but notice the huge mirror in the ceiling over the king-size bed. The drawers of the bedside tables yielded little to Nate; a box of condoms, several sex toys, and a small silver-plated .32 cal. automatic which he placed in his pocket.

The two walk-in closets were only slightly more interesting. One contained women's clothing. The other contained four men's suits, half a dozen shirts, a tie rack, and two pairs of hand-made cowboy boots. On a shelf, Nate found a sawed-off 20-gauge shotgun with the stock cut down to a pistol grip and two boxes of shells. A *nasty piece of work*, he thought as he collected the gun and two boxes of shells.

The huge bathroom with a sunken tub three times the size of a normal tub contained two sink areas. One obviously for a female, the other for a male, set up with shaving gear and after-shave lotion, the scent of which was vaguely familiar, but Nate couldn't place it. Altogether his search of the master bedroom and the smaller bedroom, revealed no clue as to the identity of the male occupant. Nate returned to the living room and found the female lying face down on the couch with her hands bound behind her back by Roberto's belt and his bandana in her mouth. He was sheepishly standing by her side and speaking Spanish to her. Whatever he was saying, (and he never explained) had its effect because she gradually stopped struggling. He removed the gag and belt and helped her sit up. Even in her disheveled state, she was striking and neither man could bring themselves to threaten harm.

Roberto said to her, in Spanish. "Can you tell us please where is El Tigre?"

The young lady replied also in Spanish, "I know no one by that name."

"How about Emilo Zuma?" asked Roberto.

"Ni idea."

"Do you know the location of his ranch?" asked Roberto in Spanish.

"Ni idea."

"Do you know the whereabouts of the blond American woman El Tigre kidnapped?" asked Roberto in the same manner.

"Ni idea."

With each reply the young lady looked both Roberto and Nate directly in the eye. If she were lying, she made a very convincing showing otherwise. They both tended to believe her, which left them with their only chance to find El Tigre with the two Mexican guards.

They pulled out all telephone lines and led the woman back to the master bedroom where they used ripped-up pillowcases to tie her up. They left her on the bed, closed the door and wedged it shut with a wooden brace they had worked free from supporting a hall closet shelf.

“That should hold her long enough for us to get out of town,” commented Nate. Before leaving they disassembled the shotgun and automatic and threw the parts into the back alley.

As Nate and Roberto returned to where Hatch was guarding the prone prisoners, Nate looked at them expectantly,

“One of these guys has to tell us what we need.”

With that Roberto grabbed up the chubby one and half-dragged and half herded him to the far end of the vestibule where he began speaking to him in Spanish, while slapping him in the face every time he said, *“No se.”*

Finally, after his lips were bleeding, his face red and stinging and with tears flowing from his eyes, the chubby Mexican crossed himself, clasped his hands together as in prayer and *said, “Te lo dire. “Pero soy hombre muerto”*

Roberto replied, *“Eres hombre muerto a menas que de cir la veidad.”*

The threat worked and the battered man began rapidly speaking in Spanish. When he had finished, Roberto grabbed him by his collar and flung him at the feet of Tom and Nate. The eyes of the guard, the other captive, grew so large his face could barely contain them, as he witnessed this, but he said nothing.

With a wicked smile, Roberto explained, “The chubby one told me he was a dead man if he talked. I told him he was a dead man if he didn’t. He talked.” Roberto then turned to both captives and said, *“No decir nada. Si usted habla eres hombre muerto! Comprende?”*

Both men, their eyes huge, their faces almost white, blurted simultaneously, *“Si, Si, Senor.”*

Roberto turned to his companions, “Okay, the chubby guy is the assistant manager, we can probably believe what he said. He confirms Zuma owns the club, but he hasn't seen him in weeks. He claims to know nothing of the woman Zuma's men are supposed to have grabbed. He doesn't know who owns or lives in the apartment. Whoever it is, he shows up every now and then with his own bodyguards. No one is allowed to go upstairs. He has seen Zuma get into the elevator once or twice. He seemed nervous each time. The guard at the door is not one of Zuma's men. He belongs to the one they call 'Big Man.' No one wants to look at him when he comes around. All this guy can say is this Big Man is big around but not overly tall. The girl belongs to him. She is the third one in two years. He doesn't know her, has never spoken to her. Their orders are to give her anything she asks for. The word is Zuma is at his ranch – he's never been there but has heard its about fourteen or fifteen miles west of Juarez off the main highway several miles. It's very big and is called *Rancho del Aguila Real*, the Golden Eagle Ranch. He says we take Mexican Highway 45 past the airport and hit Highway 2 and turn right at a Pemex station and a little store. There are a number of houses, but the place has no name. We stay on Highway 2 for some eight or nine miles until we reach this place, then we follow the gravel road to the ranch. He says that's all he can tell us – all he knows. I believe him."

Roberto turned his attention back to the two captives and said, "I know you understand English good enough, so I am only going to say this once." With that he drew his pistol and slowly moved it from one man to the next. Their eyes followed the movement of the weapon as though they were hypnotized. "We are going out the front door to our car. You two are coming with us. If you do as I say and cooperate, no harm will come to you. Understand?" Both men vigorously nodded their heads. "Okay," said Roberto, "Behave yourselves and you will be released outside the city. Now you," pointing his handgun at the heavy-set one, "Will walk to my left." "You," he said while swinging his pistol around to point to the other prisoner, "Will walk on that man's left side." *(Pointing to Nate.)* The subject of Roberto's gesture lurched backward and raised his hands to his face as if they would shield him from a bullet. Quickly though, he nodded.

"Now, I want to be very clear about this," said Roberto and he continued to swing his weapon back and forth between the two men. "Any attempt to attract attention or escape and you will be dead a dead man! *Comprende*?" Both men nodded their understanding even as they recoiled in fear.

The group descended in the elevator and passed through the club and out the front door without incident. They quickly walked to their rented car and Roberto raised the trunk lid and gestured for the two men to get in. At first, they were reluctant, but when Nate and Roberto reminded them of the vulnerability of their position by ramming their pistols into their respective necks, they meekly crawled into the trunk of the car.

The three, with Hatch at the wheel, had no difficulty making their way out of the city. After several miles, Hatch pulled to the side of the road. As the car rolled to a stop, Hatch turned and looked into the rear seat at Roberto.

"We're going to let these two guys live, right?"

"Listen, as quick as these two guys can find a telephone, they're gonna report us. You don't know these people," Roberto answered, as if explaining something to a simpleton.

Hatch, with a hard stare, answered, "Chaves, the guy in Reynosa, didn't say anything, he kept his word."

"Chaves was not a cartel guy, he was like an independent contractor, he wasn't bound to the cartel. Besides, no one saw us talk to him, so he was safe," replied Roberto. Hatch just continued to stare. "Okay, Okay, you Americans and your sensibilities. These guys walk. I just hope we don't all regret it." said Roberto. Whereupon he sprang out of the car, slamming the door. He went to the rear and as the trunk lid began to open, he thrust this pistol into the faces of the two, by now almost comatose, men. The assistant manager squealed out,

"No! No!"

Ignoring this outburst, Roberto calmly said, "I remind you one more time, you talk to no one."

"Si,Si, we not talk," they said in unison as they scrambled from the trunk. "Off you go then." Without another word the two began running back the way they had come.

Chapter 26 – Into the Tiger's Lair

Dawn was creeping over the arid landscape as they reached the Pemex station. Hatch again pulled to the side of the road just short of it. Turning to the others, he said, "Okay guys, what now? I don't think we can attempt a rescue in broad daylight."

Nate said, "you're right but maybe we ought to scout up ahead before it gets dark."

Roberto disagreed saying, "I think we better stay close to where we are. We have no idea where El Tigre has people. We could stumble upon one by accident and blow this whole deal."

"Well, all right, but what are we going to do till night?" asked Nate.

"How about we do this," suggested Hatch. "Let's gas up the car at the Pemex station and since it has a convenience store, we buy some water and food and then drive up the road until we find a spot to conceal the car. Then we wait there till dark."

"I agree," said Roberto.

"Let's do it then," said Nate.

After gassing up and buying some food, they drove down the gravel road several miles until a clump of honey mesquite and Mexican palo verde offered some hope of concealment. They spent a miserable day waiting for sundown while the temperature hovered over 105 degrees F. Finally, the sun began to fade. They drank some water, checked their weapons, and set out in single file spaced intervals along the road. The tense threat of danger, the smell of his own body odor, the darkness, the slog with weapons, all served to bring back unpleasant memories of Viet Nam to Nate. This time though, it was different, this time it was personal. This time it was not about duty-this time it was for love. This time the primeval, gut-wrenching fear was not for himself, it was for his wife. He knew he could never find peace unless he could bring Jen home. Sundown brought little relief from the heat and soon they were each drenched in sweat. After what they reasoned to be a mile or so, they left the road and moved through the rough countryside but keeping parallel to the road.

After an exhausting forty-five minutes, the night closed in, no lights, except the stars, which were barely visible through the clouds. In the distant foreground they suddenly noticed a light which appeared and disappeared according to the heat waves, and which seemed to be located on the road ahead. Pursued by insects of all kinds, they plowed through the darkness occasionally stumbling over a low-lying bush or rock. Once Hatch sprawled full-length upon the rocky soil and into a cactus.

"Damn! Son-of-a-bitch! Ouch! Shit!" yelled Hatch, as he extracted himself from the thorny embrace. Such blue language coming from the strait-laced Latter Day Saint was so unexpected and unusual for him that Nate and Roberto had to snicker. "These things hurt-it's not funny," said Hatch indignantly, while he clinched his fists and stared at his companions.

"Whoa, there buddy," said Nate. "Sorry man. We know it hurt and we're not making light of it. It's just so out of character for you to talk that way, that it seemed funny. Really sorry if you took it the wrong way."

"Yeah, what he said," said Roberto.

After a few minutes, Hatch now somewhat mollified and obviously trying to regain his normal good humor, finally said in a very soft voice, "I guess, if I were in your shoes, I might have seen some humor in it too." With that he turned and resumed their trek and didn't look back.

Nate thought, as he hurried after Hatch, *I could kick myself usually a laugh eases tension but instead might have just create more.*

Eventually, they drew close enough to the light to discern its source. It was located over a metal gate and under its glare sat a stone guardhouse manned by two machine gun toting dark skinned men. The light also revealed a highwire fence running off in either direction topped by coils of razor wire.

As they crouched breathlessly in the still night, Nate whispered, "Guess we're here."

They retreated a safe distance to have a council of war.

"What now?" said Hatch as the quarter moon slowly peeped through the scattered clouds and cast a silvery glow over the parched landscape.

"I think we need to find a dry creek," said Roberto. "This country is full of these places where when it rains, they are like rivers and, in a few days, when things dry out, they are just depressions in the ground. Even simple barbed-wire fences leave gaps where they cross these creek beds. It is a full-time job to keep these gaps fenced up for most ranchers. This fence is a professional job. I'd be willing to bet that these cartel hired guns are no good at repairing a fence, let alone one like this. In fact, I doubt that even vaqueros, who are pretty good with barbed wire fences, could do much with this one. "

So, keeping low so they could not be seen from the road, they moved off along the fence guided by the slivers of moonlight. After about seventy feet, they came to a depression in the ground. It was some three feet deep and about five wide and extended beneath the fence and off into the darkness beyond in both directions. They clambered down into the bottom and Roberto pushed debris out of the way to reveal the bottom of the fence. There was an opening of some three or four inches between the creek bed and the last fence strand. Roberto tried digging with his hands, but the crusty bottom was unyielding.

"We need something to dig with," he said, as he crawled upon the bank.

They separated and began searching.

Hatch called softly, "Over here."

He'd found a dead mesquite tree with its trunk halved by some long-ago lightning strike. The three tugged and pulled at the tree but it refused to surrender its crippled limb.

Finally, Nate suggested, "Let's sit on it and swing up and down."

They did. The six hundred or so pounds coupled with the swaying motion had the desired effect. Gradually, the tree began to split further and then after more pulling and tugging the trunk yielded its smaller half. Roberto made the final tug and was rewarded with a six-foot-long stout piece of mesquite wood pointed at one end.

Roberto immediately began stabbing the limb into the ground beneath the lowest wire rung of the fence. In vain; the ground was akin to concrete. As the other two looked on, Roberto unzipped his fly and left a damp spot on the ground.

"Come on you guys, help me out here," he said. Nate and Hatch did as they were bid and gradually Roberto's efforts began to tell. The ground beneath the surface was dry but not as hard as the surface. Eventually then a trench formed under the wire that allowed the three to slide under the fence. As they moved away from the fence in the direction of the driveway, the halcyon evening was abruptly pierced by a sound that caused the hair on the back of their necks to rise. The sound drew nearer and louder as other voices joined in.

"Wolves?" asked Hatch.

"Either that or something just as bad," said Roberto. "We need to get back on the other side of that fence fast!"

They turned and began running back the way they had come but all too soon they were overtaken by a pack of five or six huge mastiffs, their mouths open and drooling with unearthly sounds arising from their throats. Strangely, however, as fierce as was their demeanor, they made no move to attack but were content to circle the group so as to prevent their movement. The explanation for this bizarre behavior soon became apparent. Two pickup trucks with deer spotting lights roared up. The passengers sprang from the trucks and the passenger from the lead truck aimed his machine gun at the three and shouted.

"Levanta tus manos" and "suelten sus armos!"

"He says to raise our hands and drop our guns," Roberto translated. "I suggest we do so."

With waves of their weapons, the guards instructed them to hold out their hands to be tied. They were loaded onto the rear of one of the trucks with a guard facing them and his machine gun pointed at them. The truck fell in line behind the other as they both gained the graveled driveway after enduring the intervening scabious terrain. Shortly they roared into a large, paved parking area in front of a massive Mexican hacienda-style dwelling. Lights were on all over and the front door was flanked by two machine gun toting guards. The three were roughly ushered indoors where they struggled to regain their sight in the large brightly lit room that they found themselves in.

After some fifteen or twenty minutes, El Tigre himself appeared. His rotund figure was draped in a scarlet silk robe over matching pajamas. On his feet were tasseled slippers. His hair was mussed, and his attitude was decidedly inhospitable.

"So, you three dead men finally made it here," he said. "I've been waiting for you ever since you let my men out of the trunk of your car. Did you not think they would immediately notify me of your coming?" What fools! Unfortunately, I have business out of town and I cannot enjoy your company. But when I return, the day after tomorrow, we shall have a *persegun o cazar* as we say or, a chase in your language. We take your clothes, leave you your boots, we give you a bottle of water and an hour's start and then we cut loose the dogs. We follow on horseback. My men look forward to it. When the dogs are done, we roast a steer or goat and drink a lot of tequila." During these biting remarks, Roberto unabashedly glared at Hatch. Hatch, obviously greatly embarrassed, just stood there with his face tuning a shade of red.

"Where's my wife?" shouted Nate. "What have you done with her?"

"Not to worry, she is safe. I haven't had a chance yet to visit with her but, after the chase, I will have time to enjoy her before I hand her over to my men."

"You big fat piece of shit! I'll kill you," yelled Nate as he leaped for the man. However, Nate's lunge was cut short by a violent blow to the rear of his head from a gun butt of one of the guards. All went black and then as his sight slowly returned, he found himself sprawled at the feet of the fat man, whose natural impulse was to kick Nate in the face.

The kick was more an embarrassment than it was painful since El Tigre was wearing house shoes. Still, it stung and burst Nate's lip. The acid taste of his blood was more than enough motivation for him to do a quick roll and bounce to his feet. However, quick as he was, the guards were standing close on each side and subdued him before he could get to El Tigre.

"Take them to the hut – I'll deal with them when I return. I'm going back to bed," said the chubby one as he walked out of the room.

The three were frog-marched out the front door and some thirty yards to the rear to an adobe hut with a dirt floor and narrow glassless windows up high on three sides.

Roberto spoke to their guards in Spanish asking to have their arms freed. After all he pointed out, they had no weapons, were outnumbered, and would be locked up. Surely these people were not afraid of them, were they?

After a short discussion, one of the guards produced a switch blade and cut their ties. They were then shoved into the black interior of the hut and the door slammed shut.

They lay on the dirt floor exhausted. Even after their eyes adjusted to the darkness, there was nothing they could see. The narrow windows were of little help since the night now was cloudy. They felt their way around the interior walls and smelled rather than felt a bucket in one corner. Other than that, there was nothing in the hut. After a short discussion, they all agreed there was nothing they could do now. They needed rest and would see what the morrow brought. They lay on the dirt and tried to sleep.

Chapter 27 – Captives

LT, you o.k.? Nate is semi-conscious as a result of the RPG blast that exploded the head of his RTO Delaney. He scarcely feels the hands of Weber, his platoon sergeant, as he gently shakes him. Slowly, Nate becomes aware of his surroundings – the lush green all around, the stench of rotting plants and wood from the nearby swamp, the buzz of insects and finally the coppery scent of human blood. He almost retches as he becomes aware of Delaney's cranial matter and blood soaking into his camos. He slowly moves his arms and legs. Pain hits him from his lower left side and mid-back.

Without being asked, Weber says, "Purple heart special. Looks like shrapnel got you, lots of blood."

"I'm fine," Nate says as his sergeant is giving him first aid. Nate takes a deep breath or two and his mind begins to clear, and he becomes aware of the sounds of small arms fire.

Nate turns to Weber, "I'm okay – just a little concussed. Any other casualties?"

"Not yet but the VC have us pinned down and are moving in. Must be a battalion, their mortars are starting to range us."

"Where are the 6 O's?"

"I got one at point and one at our six."

"Good, have the point 6 O pull back, rear m.g. give covering fire, let's get the hell out of here."

Nate fumbles for the radio near Delaney's body, turns it on and thank God it still works. Nate orders up a couple of gunships to give them covering fire as they withdraw and a couple of helos to extract them. He designates the LZ where they were dropped off earlier. The men moved by squads past him on their bellies or hands and knees no one wanting to be a hero – just wanting to get back home. He counts the men as they move past him. All accounted for. The body of Delaney has been placed in a body bag and is being pulled along the trail. The mortar bursts are getting closer. The VC can't see them but they know generally where they are. Now and then Nate hears short bursts from the machine gun up front. There is return fire from several directions but none of it real close. As the men move down the trail and away from the trees, the foliage, mainly elephant grass, becomes taller and thicker so that now they are able to stand up about half ways. Movement is now easier and quicker.

Nate is the last of the column and while waiting for everyone to pass, he has now allowed a sizable gap between himself and the last of his men. He decides to pick it up a bit when all of a sudden, a shape materializes up ahead. It's a thin body clad in black. His head is turned away from Nate as he is intent on finding the rear of the withdrawing file.

Silently, Nate checks his M16 to be sure the safety is off, and he moves the fire control to full auto. Nate is standing still and begins moving his rifle to bear when the VC suddenly turns to face him. He's a skinny kid, maybe thirteen or fourteen. He's armed with an AK-47 which he is beginning to swing toward Nate. Nate hesitates for a fraction of a second – just a kid.

Nate's rifle is waist high, and the VC's weapon is now lining up on Nate. Nate's brain disengages and muscle memory takes over. His finger squeezes the trigger, and his rifle spouts out a short burst which strikes the kid center mass, and he is dead before he hits the ground. He had been able to pull his trigger before being struck by Nate's burst, but his weapon was not on target and his shots went harmlessly up in the air.

Nate steps over the body and hurries after his men.

Nate wakes with a start. He is drenched with sweat. Been a while since he has had the dream. He guessed recent events had triggered it.

"You okay?" asked Tom.

"Yeah, just a bad dream."

"The old one?"

"Yeah, thought I was through with it – guess not."

The sun was barely an orange glow on the eastern horizon but already there was enough light to make out dim shapes. However, except for the three of them there was nothing to see. Their area of confinement was about twelve by twelve with a dirt floor. The windows were too high to see out of but Nate found the slop bucket in a far corner, emptied out whatever unsavory contents it contained and turned it upside down, to serve as a perch, beneath a window on the side where he reckoned the house was. He balanced himself and was able to look out.

Nothing was moving. Then as the sun rose above the horizon, he saw two armed men trudging into the back door of the main house. Perimeter guards, he thought. Then out of the corner of his eye he counted seven more coming from his left. As he moved as far to his right as he could, he was able to see a low-lying building from which the group had left. Quarters for the guards, he figured.

He stepped down from his perch and shared his discovery with Tom and Roberto. "At least eleven hard cases," he said, "counting the two at the gate. It's six-thirty – must be guard change. I bet there's no perimeter security in day time. He depends on the gate guards."

"Makes sense," said Tom. "Anybody have a plan?"

"Not a plan, but a suggestion," said Roberto. "I say we take no action until the fat shit leaves on his trip. He's known to travel with at least five guards, a driver, and a guard in his car, and a driver and at least two others in the trail car. By waiting, we even the odds considerably."

They all agreed. Further discussion was interrupted by Nate returning to his post.

After a while, he said, "Two guys in a pickup rounding the corner of the house. Probably headed for the gate." His assumption was proven correct when after about twenty minutes, the same pickup returned with two different men inside.

After a while, a group of men left the back door of the house and headed for the flat roofed building. One man carrying a bucket broke off and headed in their direction carrying an AK-47 in one hand. "Looks like breakfast guys!" said Nate as he stepped down from his perch and lay down on the floor near the wall opposite the door. Tom and Roberto had already taken their places.

A few minutes later there was a banging on the door and a voice said in broken English, "Want food?" Back from door! Make *problema, no las comida*!" There was the sudden appearance of a shaft of sunlight as a panel was opened on the door and a face appeared. Apparently satisfied that it was safe, there followed the rattle of a lock, and the squeak of rusted hinges. The door was eased open a few inches and a gun barrel appeared. Being reassured that it was safe, the man advanced a few feet into the hut, placed the bucket down and without a word retreated, slammed the door and locked it.

Several hours later, Nate observed two black Lincoln automobiles drive up to the front of the house. Directly he saw

El Tigre exit the house and enter the first car. Another man entered the passenger seat while two others entered the second vehicle. Immediately both cars started down the long drive and were out of sight in seconds.

"Well," Nate mused, "if our count is right, we have four gunmen to deal with and I'm not concerned about the two gate guards."

"Yeah," agreed Tom. "And if they maintain their nighttime perimeter, all four will be sleepy and tired."

"I'm betting they maintain their routine," put in Roberto, "At least they'll go through the motions, after all, they have a captive to guard. I have a surprise for the guy bringing us breakfast tomorrow morning," continued Roberto as he slipped off his right boot and yanked out the leather insole. He pulled out a very thin flexible stiletto. "A modified version of the SAS Sheffield Fairbain – Sykes dagger," Roberto explained. "It's razor sharp on either side. I'll take out the guy who delivers our food in the morning."

Having made their plans, the three spent a restless day and night in anticipation of the morrow. "*Like racehorses*," thought Nate, "*waiting for the bell.*" Although summer had passed, fall in these parts was still hot, especially in the small hut with a tin roof. As the afternoon temperature soared, the three were only able to find some relief by shedding most of their clothing only to scramble to put them back on as the sun disappeared from view. They waited in vain for an evening meal, especially water. The small bottle of water left them in the morning had long since disappeared into parched throats.

There had been no further guard changes so the three assumed the gate guards worked twelve-hour shifts, one man standing guard while the other slept. As darkness descended and lights came on in the big house, Nate had seen the shapes of the guards enter and, after a while, leave to return to their quarters. Nate heard the dogs being let out and saw the two outside guards begin their rounds. Lights in the big house went out around ten o'clock and afterwards, except for the soft sounds of the wind and occasional howl of a dog or coyote, all was quiet.

The three were awake well before dawn, having slept little during the chilly night. From his adopted position, Nate observed the guard change and finally the approach of their breakfast. He quickly lay down next to Tom at the far wall. Near them were Roberto's trousers tucked into his boots facing the door. Again, the shaft of sunlight, the rattle of the lock, the squeak of the hinges, and the gradual opening of the door. The guard entered behind his AK-47 and bent down to place the bucket on the ground and while his eyes were directed downward, Roberto sprang from behind the door and with one rapid movement, slashed the guard's throat. As soon as he fell, Roberto was removing his clothing.

Having donned the guard's clothes, Roberto said, "I'll go and bring back the other guards. We'll lock them up in here."

With repulsion, but knowing it to be necessary, Tom and Nate drag the dead guard's naked body to the far back wall of the shed. Then with stress mounting they took turns upon the window perch and watch Roberto as he moves cat-like from the shed, across the open space and into the shadow of the barracks building. Without being aware of it, both Nate and Tom are literally holding their breath knowing, as they do, that at any moment, Roberto could be spotted. One shout, one outcry could bring superior numbers and superior weapons to bear and all their hopes for escape, their plans to capture El Tigre and to rescue Jen, even their very lives would be forfeited. As they watch, Roberto enters a doorway to the barracks and is lost to sight. In vain they strain to hear gunshots, nothing. All is quiet. They wonder, *Is this good news or bad news*?

Roberto slipped into what was a sort of day room and as he entered the next room it was, as he expected, a barracks room with double layer bunks lining the walls. The building, as Roberto noticed, was built of thick adobe bricks. Being sure the sound would not carry to the gate, he loosened a long burst from his weapon, chewing up lockers and empty bunks.

As the dazed sleepy-eyed men rolled out of their bunks, Roberto shouted to the startled men, *"Arriba! Arriba!, Get up!" Manos arriba! Hands Up!" Out to Cobertizo!"*

Still about half asleep the dazed men most of them in their under shorts, one or two butt naked, meekly followed orders and offered no resistance as they were herded into the shed. Roberto then handed his weapon to Tom to guard their captives as he dressed in his own clothing.

"Okay," Nate said, as he locked the shed. "So far so good. I'm going to the bunk-house, I'll gather the weapons and meet you two at the back door. Hopefully the household staff are not armed but if they are, and want a fire fight, at least we'll be able to hold our own."

Shortly, all three, now armed with AK-47's, stood at the back door of the main building.

"I'll go straight in," Nate whispered tensely. "Roberto go left and Tom, you go right." They both nodded and released the safeties on their weapons. "Okay, here we go," said Nate, as he landed his right boot on the back door which splintered at the latch and swung inward. Nate, followed closely by the other two, sprang inside and all swept the room with their AK's.

Chapter 28 – Rescue

Fractions of a second later, with the sound of the back door shattering still in their ears, their senses were startled by a piercing scream and another loud crash. All three rotated toward the noise to see a matronly Mexican woman with her hands over her heart and a dish towel and pieces of a glass pitcher lying at her feet. Her face was drained of color and her eyes were larger than silver dollars.

"*No dispares! No dispares,*" she was saying. Roberto told her in Spanish that they were not going to shoot her and that they were police.

"Habla Ingles?"

"*Si, unpoco.*"

"Where is the American woman?"

"Up the stairs."

"Is she all right," Nate demanded. "Take us to her. She's my wife."

"*Si, si,* is okay. I take care of her. We are friends."

Just then an elderly gray-haired man rushed into the kitchen. "Manuela are you okay?" he asked. He skidded to a stop upon seeing the three-armed men. He regained his composure when Manuela told him they were police.

"This is Caesar, my husband," she said. "The fat man and his bandits took us from our village, which they burned. They won't let us leave and make us work for them. Come," she added to Nate. "I will take you to your wife. She is very brave. She love you very much."

The two of them climbed the stairs with Manuela leading. They went down a long hallway and she finally paused in front of a door.

"It is locked," said Manuela. "One of the *traficante de drogas* had to always open it for me."

Nate tried the doorknob, it was locked.

"Jen," he shouted, "it's me, I've come to take you home. Are you okay?"

"Nate, is that you? I knew you'd come. I'm all right."

"Stand back from the door sweetheart, I'm going to kick it down." With that Nate swung a boot against the door. It didn't move. "Okay, I'm going to have to shoot the lock, please get in a far corner." A short burst from the AK-47 blew the door into a ragged image of its former self. Another kick from Nate and the door crumbled inward and he was inside the room sweeping Jen up into his arms. Between the tears and kisses, nothing either said was recognizable.

Finally, Jen broke free and moved to Manuela. "Thank you, you kept my spirit up. I don't know if I could have kept my mind without you," she said, as she hugged Manuela, who also with tears in her eyes, hugged her back.

As they joined the others, Hatch came forward and hugged Jen – he might have had tears in his eyes also. Hand in hand then, Nate introduced her to Roberto, who, instead of shaking her extended hand, bowed and kissed it. Caesar just bowed.

Bringing everyone's attention back to their precarious situation, Hatch said "Caesar, did you hear when the boss will be due back?"

"No, he tried never to talk where Manuela and I can hear."

"But you did hear things," said Hatch guessing.

"*Si*," said Caesar, with a shy grin. "He not as smart as he thinks. Manuela and me listen and we watch. We be careful so he not know. Most times, he returns at dusk. We tell you everything we know, *nosotras mucho egradecido.*"

"I think right now, that's all we need to know," said Nate, breaking into the conversation. "I am very thankful to you and your wife for taking care of Jen."

"Is Nada El placer es nuestro. You saved our lives. *Pideme lo que quieras."*

"Well, thank you," said Nate, "but, as I said, I think we have all we need now."

"So, we post a guard and the rest make themselves as comfortable as they can," said Tom. "I'll take the first post," as he grabbed a chair and dragged it to a front window.

Nate and Jen occupied one of the leather couches, holding on to each other and speaking softly. Roberto lay down on another couch and was soon asleep. Manuela and Caesar went to the kitchen and began preparing a meal.

Time, being its fickle self, refused to move, or at least, that is the way it felt. After they had finished eating, Roberto took over the watch and conversation soon faded out. Each person with his or her private thoughts. Finally, near dusk, after an interminable day, Roberto suddenly said, "Here he comes."

"Caesar," said Nate, "What's the usual routine when the boss returns from a trip."

"Well, if it's late like this, he'll be hungry and so will his guards. Usually both cars are parked out front, and the boss allows his men to come in the front door with him. They go straight to the kitchen while he goes to his study and has a drink and reviews any correspondence. Most of the men leave their big guns on the table by the door. When they finish eating, they collect their weapons and return to the cars. They park them in the garage and then they go to their quarters. The boss will then, when he is ready, seat himself at the big table in the dining room and he will be served his special meal by myself."

"Okay then," Nate ordered. "Jen, you, Manuela, and Caesar go upstairs and lock yourselves in a far bedroom and don't come out until I come for you."

"Promise you'll be careful. I love you so much," said Jen.

"I love you, too," said Nate, "And I'll be careful. Now please go."

Nate turned to Roberto and Tom. "Based on what Caesar told us, I suggest we hide until the guards have laid down their weapons and gone into the kitchen. They'll be milling around wondering where Caesar and Manuela are and why their dinner isn't ready. Tom, I suggest that you and Roberto surprise them and make them prisoners. I'll hit Zuma in his study. Okay?"

Tom and Roberto nodded agreement; Tom went out the back door and Roberto stepped into the pantry. Nate went to the study and hid behind the door.

They had not long to wait. Within minutes there was the sound of loud motors, then braking followed by car doors being slammed. Spanish and laughing.

Then the voice of Zuma, "Caesar where are you?" "Manuela, you *vaca perezosa*, get my men food!" Zuma went to the bar and returned with two bottles of tequila. "Here," he told his men, "Whet your appetites. I am sure those two *el Palurdos* will be here shortly if they know what's good for them." This was said in a mixture of English and Spanish, which his men seemed to understand. "*Disfautar, tengo trabajo que hacer.*"

With that, Zuma left the kitchen and went to his study. After turning on the lights, he walked behind his desk and to the credenza behind it. With his back still to the door, he poured himself a tall glass of Laphroaig ten-year-old single malt scotch whiskey. He was startled when Nate shut the door. He turned quickly and saw Nate. His eyes bulged and his face blanched with shock. The glass of whiskey tumbled from his hand as he eyed the AK-47 held unerringly by Nate and pointed at his center mass.

"You – you, where did you come from? How did you get in here?"

"Shut up and put your hands behind your head; lock your fingers together and come with me," said Nate, as he opened the study door. He glanced toward the great room and was relieved to see the guards lying on the floor while Tom held his AK-47 on them while Roberto walked among them using their own belts to bind their arms behind them. With his attention thus diverted, Nate failed to pat down Zuma for a weapon. A mistake that later almost proves fatal.

As Nate followed Zuma out of the study door, the heel of his right boot, which had been loosened when he kicked in the door, slipped on the transition between the study carpet and the tile of the hallway. This momentarily caused Nate to lose his focus so that his weapon strayed from its target. Zuma, realizing this as his chance to escape, made a wild dash for the front door. While on the dead run, he attempted to draw his automatic (which Nate had inadvertently failed to discover) from his shoulder holster but was slowed in doing so because his snug fitted double breasted suit coat was fully buttoned. When he was finally able to free his pistol, he was almost at the door and had only time to fire at where Nate had last been. Fortunately for Nate, he had regained his balance and had moved to his right so that the round from Zuma's pistol barely grazed his left shoulder. It hurt like hell and drew blood but did no real damage. Meanwhile, Zuma was out the door and heading for one of the parked Lincolns. Roberto and Tom were unable to use their weapons for fear of hitting what at present were, noncombatants.

Nate yelled, “Roberto, prisoners! Tom, with me,” as he burst through the door in pursuit of the fleeing Zuma, who by now had reached the nearest Lincoln and was pulling away with wheels spinning and gravel flying.

Tom took the wheel of the remaining Lincoln while Nate jumped into the near side passenger door and hopped over the seat into the passenger seat even as Tom was gunning the big car’s motor and the dry twilight evening’s quiet was assaulted by the harsh sounds of its huge engine. The taillights of Zuma’s vehicle appeared dimly like two red fireflies jumping and dancing in some wildly improbably choreographed performance.

The weather just then joined in and added to the mad scene. Brilliant slashes of heat lightning lit up the darkness as bright as day only to retreat into tenebrosity once again. The effect was altogether unnatural. The accompanying thunder could not be heard above the noise of the powerful engine and the road noise.

Gravel and dirt were flying about hitting the windshield and making loud pinging noises on the sides of the car and its under carriage. Vision was becoming a problem as was stability because while the small ruts in the gravel driveway presented no problem at normal speed, at eighty miles an hour, they were sufficient to cause a driver to lose control.

Tom, with his FBI training, was clearly the superior driver to Zuma, who for the last decade had been chauffeured around. Tom steadily gained on him. Then the two cars were side by side, each driver trying to swing over and strike the opposite vehicle while trying to keep control of his own. Down the dust-obscured road they went like two giant beetles butting and bouncing with neither having the advantage. Finally, when they had almost reached the gate, Tom stomped on the accelerator and viciously spun his steering wheel so that the rear of his Lincoln struck a crushing blow to the front of Zuma's.

Zuma lost control and his car went careening off sideways directly into the guardhouse at the gate. There was a loud crash, a flash of flame, a spiral of dark smoke and a loud explosion. In minutes the automobile and guardhouse resembled a Viking funeral pyre. Nothing would survive it.

Tom also had lost control of his automobile which made several complete circles as Tom fought to keep it upright. It finally came to rest against the perimeter fence. The motor was still running while the dust began to settle. Nate looked at Tom. Tom looked at Nate. They were each ashen faced.

They sat in silence, neither knowing for how long, until finally Tom said, "Guess I'd better get us back to the house, they might be worried about us." Each nodded to the other with just the shadow of a smile.

When they arrived back at the house, Tom and Nate dismounted and with shaky legs made it inside.

Faced with all the expectant faces, Nate said, "We chased Zuma all the way to the gate. Tom managed to bump his car causing him to lose control. Zuma's car crashed into the guard hut and everything went up in flames. There aren't any survivors."

Though relieved to be free of the monster that was Zuma, there was no rejoicing just a feeling of relief, after all there were three men dead.

Jen broke the silence. "Nate, you're hurt." she said, as blood oozed from his shoulder, soaking his shirt. "You need to come with me. Manuela, can you find something for a bandage? Also, something I can use to sew up this wound?" Nate made no protest as the wound in his shoulder was throbbing painfully.

"Si, I get first aid kit. Fat man keep it in case someone gets hurt."

With Nate in tow, Jen and Manuela vanished into the kitchen.

"Now, Nate, take off your shirt," said Jen.

"Jen, just get me a band aid and I'm okay. The bullet just nicked me," said Nate.

"Well, it nicked you all right "said Jen as she surveyed the wound." "It's a pretty deep gash and needs to be closed up. Not to worry, I've sewed up a bunch of cats and dogs after surgery."

"Yeah, but I'm not a cat or dog," said Nate.

Paying him no mind, Jen dug into the kit handed her by Manuela. Finding what she needed, she cleansed the wound and sutured it up. "There now." she said, as she applied a bandage. "We need to keep this clean and soon you'll be good as new."

"Meow, meow," said Nate

"If you can act silly, I guess you are all right now." said Jen.

At this point, Roberto entered from the rear door, grimly ebullient just as the thunder and lightning crashed overhead and rain began to patter down.

"I locked the *pendejos* in the hut," he explained. "What of El Tigre-did he get away?"

"Not even close," said Nate. "He's probably burning in hell right now."

"Hey Nate, take a sip or two of this, might ease the pain. I liberated Zuma's scotch," said Tom, somewhat shaky himself.

Nate took the proffered bottle and took a couple of long drinks. "I don't know if it helps, he said, "but it sure doesn't hurt."

"So, where's Roberto?" asked Tom.

"I saw him heading for Zuma's study," said Jen.

They found Roberto in Zuma's study before a wall safe. He had his ear pressed to the dial while his fingers slowly rotated it from side to side. All at once, with a grin and a flash of his white teeth, the door opened.

"What kind of a cop are you?" asked Tom.

"The resourceful kind," replied Roberto, as he was pulling a stack of bank notes from the safe and stacking them on Zuma's desk. "Must be over seventy thousand American in here," he added. "Zuma must have the rest of his money stashed elsewhere."

"Yeah, this is chump change for him," said Tom. "Probably got a lot in safety deposit boxes or overseas accounts. Some invested in legit businesses."

"So, how do you want to divide this up?" asked Roberto.

"None for me," Tom shook his head.

"Me neither," Nate also refused, but he was struck by a thought. "I say we let Caesar and Manuela take what they want, and you keep the rest, I know your government doesn't give you the funds you need."

"Sounds fine with me," said Roberto.

When informed to take what they thought they were owed, both Caesar and Manuela refused.

"Is blood money," protested Manuela.

"Money is money," Roberto replied. "It has no conscience and no memory. You were worked here as slaves, it is only right that you be compensated. It is a kind of justice that removes the stain."

Finally, Manuela nodded and Caesar took hold of a stack of bills.

"Enough to buy us a small farm somewhere safe," he remarked, with satisfaction.

"Also," said Tom, "take one of the pickup trucks."

"Yes, okay, we will need transportation away from this evil place," Caesar agreed.

The sudden rain shower had stopped, and the evening smelled fresh and clean. To Jen, Manuella and Caesar, it also smelled of freedom. Caesar parked a pickup truck in front and Manella began saying their good-byes, first hugging Jen for a long time.

She whispered, "forget this nightmare," into Jen's ear and "Love your husband, have many children and a happy life."

Then she joined Caesar who was hosing down the truck. Then he proceeded to throw dirt on it. Next, he rummaged in the toolbox and with a ball peen hammer began knocking dents in the truck. A final blow caused a crack in the windshield.

With a self-conscious smile on his face he explained, "Now we can leave! Two old Mexicans in a new truck, we would not have gotten ten miles. Either police or bandits would have stopped us."

Manuela was already in the passenger seat. Caesar slowly climbed up into the cab, raised his hand in good-by and slowly drove off.

"They should have enough time to make it out. That noise and smoke will attract some notice from the police. Wish Caesar would drive a little faster," Tom observed.

"I guess we'd best be on our way too," said Nate. "I'd suggest we drive one of the pickups to the airport – create less questions."

"Agreed," said Roberto, "but first I am going to torch the big house and guards' quarters. The hut with the guards is far enough away so that it shouldn't catch fire."

"Why bother?" asked Tom. "Zuma's dead, he's not coming back."

"Because," Roberto looked exasperated at having to explain the obvious, "I told you this was war with the cartels, this is my own scorched earth policy."

Nate helped Jen into the second row of seats in the pickup and, as he was settling in, he gazed at her in love and wonder. She melted into his arms.

"Take me home," she said.

Epilogue

Julia McKenzie was, of course, correct, she did not go to prison. Randy Owens stayed sober long enough to negotiate a plea deal for her, ten years' probation. Somehow, she also received permission to travel. Her sojourn took her to undisclosed places and lasted several months. Upon her return, she slipped effortlessly back into her former life – charitable causes, women's bridge clubs, etc. She had discovered Edgar's money from the cartel when she found the safe deposit key taped to the bottom of his center desk drawer. She found almost two hundred thousand dollars in Edgar's safety deposit drawer. After collecting the one hundred-thousand-dollar life insurance policy on Edgar's life, she had no monetary worries for the rest of her life.

The media raised a fuss, but the D.A. blamed the judge, and the judge blamed the probation officer. No one ever got to the bottom of it. People shrugged – Valley justice.

Tony divorced his wife of twenty-three years and married Mia. Law enforcement agencies long suspected Tony of being "Mr. Big" but they could never prove it. "Mr. Big" was never caught. Tony was convicted three years later for numerous drug offenses. The D.E.A. arrested him at a makeshift landing strip on his ranch near Pharr shortly after a small single engine airplane taxied up to his sheriff's car with a load of one hundred pounds of marijuana. The sheriff claimed he leased out the land and was unaware of its use and he had, in his official capacity, simply gone out to check on an aircraft sighting. He wasn't believed.

Mia became an American citizen and spent the money left her by Tony fighting the D.E.A. forfeiture action. She continued his successful wholesale beer business.

Caesar and Manuela did buy a small citrus farm. They adopted several young children whose parents had been the victims of cartel violence and they all managed to find some degree of happiness in the simple life of working the land.

Nothing more was heard of Roberto as he returned to his vigilante life pursuit of the drug cartels.

Tom and his wife had their second child as Tom continued his rise in the FBI ranks being promoted to supervisory special agent. He and Nate continued their friendship even while he continued his unrelenting efforts to attract Nate to the FBI.

Nate and Jen returned to Austin and their respective careers. Over her protestations that she was fine, Jen yielded to the urging of Nate and her parents and attended therapy sessions for several months. Nate took care to see that he dropped her off and picked her up from work each day. When he was in trial out of town, her parents came down to stay with her and performed this routine. Jen chaffed under this smothering. Finally, one evening as she, Nate, and her parents, who were visiting, gathered for their "happy hour," she extracted the Beretta pistol from her purse.

"I am through with all this hovering around me," she announced. "I know you're doing it because you love me and want to keep me safe, but I'm full-grown and can take care of myself. I promise you I don't intend to ever be the victim again. I can't say the same for anyone who tries to make me one."

Things returned to normal and Cat recovered and resumed his nightly excursions.

Thanks and Acknowledgements

When I decided, finally, to do this project, little did I realize that the writing would be the easiest part – and that was hard enough. That it got done at all is due in large part to the help and encouragement I received from family and friends. To them I extend my heartfelt thanks and gratitude. A special few stand out:

To my daughter, Pamela Robertson, for reading the earliest version of *Ricochet* and for making helpful suggestions, especially as to the Spanish language.

To our friend Lynda Coble for typing and computer skills.

To my extraordinary wife, Kay, whose belief in the project and in me never faltered, and whose suggestions served to make this work better.

Finally, to Julia Hayden of Watercress Press, whose professionalism, knowledge and talent in large measure carried the work to fruition.

Jerry Zunker
August, 2023

www.ingramcontent.com/pod-product-compliance
Lightning Source LLC
Chambersburg PA
CBHW070543310726
48982CB00010B/1461/J
9798218263294